Lost in Wonder

LIZ CHAPMAN

D.o.l.l.
MINISTRIES

www.dollministries.com
Adelaide, South Australia
info@dollministries.com

ISBN: 9780645508666

Scripture taken from the King James Version.

Cataloguing-in-Publications entry is available from the National Library of Australia http:/catalogue.nla.gov.au

First Edition published 2023

YELLOW HEART

love stories to strengthen and inspire

For my dear friend, fellow author, and sister in Christ,

Jennifer Q. Hunt.

Thank you for believing I could.

And the heavens shall praise Thy wonders, O Lord:
Thy faithfulness also in the congregation of the saints.

Psalm 89:5

Part One

Chapter 1

NOVEMBER 1835, LONDON

Agnes was never one to search for grace, but grace found her, nonetheless. It might have even knocked on her door, had Agnes owned a door on which to knock.

In the unrelenting drizzle and blackened air of London's slums, Agnes Archibald crept from the alley where she'd spent the night. She shifted from shadows to doorways and down the streets of Cheapside, searching for a pocket to pick. All she needed was some cheap gin to ward off the cold and she wasn't about to sell herself to get it.

Heavy fog lingered over the city her parents once thought held such promise. But industry not only stole livelihoods, it stole lives. Within the first year out of the country, her naïve papa had been taken by a machine at the factory, her mam shortly after by alcohol. Three years Agnes had made her own way on these streets, from the fragile age of fourteen, and she wasn't about to give up now because of this damned cold.

She pulled her threadbare cloak around her shoulders and spotted a wink of gold in the crowd. Whoever was visiting Cheapside was well-to-do enough to own a gold pocket watch. But not for long. Agnes slipped like a phantom between the shoulders of the laboring class, her grey eyes fixed on the gentleman handing shillings to a flower merchant. If he could afford to pay good money for flowers that were alive today and dead tomorrow, then he surely wouldn't miss one measly pocket watch. He probably had one for every day of the week. And once Agnes would execute her sleight of hand, she knew just who to take it to—one who would ask no questions. Most thieves only stole what in good society they could likely afford, as selling the items thereafter drew far too much attention to themselves. But Agnes was not like most thieves. When she was forced onto the streets, she swiftly made it her mission to find those who were on the side of justice and those who were not. Even if the unscrupulous merchants tried to buy more than she was willing to sell, in time they learned not to harass Agnes Archibald. She had the rough and tumble boys of the north to thank for her bruteness, the ones who taught her a thing or two what it meant to be the only lass born to a farmer. She'd been treated as one of the boys. Though she never imagined how it might one day serve her.

Her nimble fingers reached through the bustling crowd. One click, one swipe, and the shining band would fall into her grasp as she slipped through the crowd, never to be seen again. Or at least, that was her plan. But grace it seemed had other ideas. For the very moment she attempted the steal, a vice grasped her small wrist and held her firm.

"Let me go," she shrieked, writhing and kicking against the man.

"Not until you give me back what is mine," the gentleman said calmly, leading her into a backstreet, away from the eyes of observers.

She glanced up at his iron gaze, but she couldn't hold it. "Fine. Have it! I've seen better, and I know what the likes of you do to girls in back alleys. Now, let me go."

His face visibly strained, and he held her wrist up above her head and set her against the wall. "What exactly are you accusing me of? As far as I can see, you stole from me. I am merely waiting for you to return my property."

"How can I when you've got such hold of me."

"You have two hands, miss."

Agnes' fight waned beneath his calm demeanor, and she reached into her cloak and pulled out the watch. "Now let me go."

"I could have you arrested."

Her face drained of color, though she tried to fight the effect his words had on her. She had been arrested. Once. When she was still too young to execute a decent theft. Eighteen months in the mill working from five in the morning till nine at night with nothing but gruel for breakfast and potatoes for supper was too much to bear. Her hair had only just grown back after being shorn, a disgrace that followed her and kept her from making any responsible income as a bard on the streets of London. No one wanted to hear the fables—albeit thrilling ones— from a convicted criminal of the worst kind. A woman.

"Tell me," he said, a little softer. "Why do you steal?"

"Isn't it obvious?" She laughed bitterly. "I only meant to steal a few pennies till I saw your watch in the crowd. You shouldn't wear things like that around these parts if you want to keep it."

"And you shouldn't turn to stealing."

"Well, it's either that or selling my body, so which would you recommend?"

Agnes finally met his eye with a look of steel from her own. She was a survivor. Every morning she woke more determined than the last that the day might bring change. She'd lost count of the number of times she had wanted to return home to the country, but travel was expensive and dangerous and she never had enough money to get beyond the day's needs. She had lived on cheap gin and the stale leftovers from merchants for as long as she could remember. If she could just survive long enough for change to sweep through like a fresh wind, then she would hold onto hope with a grasp as impenetrable as if she'd just stolen the crown jewels.

"I have an alternative," the gentleman said at last, finally releasing her to claim his watch. "Come and work for me as a housemaid."

Nursing her wrist to her chest, she sneered up at him. "Why would you want me to work for you? I'm no good. You said it yourself. You could have me arrested."

Curiosity rather than condemnation creased his brow, and she couldn't understand it. "What's your name?"

She rarely told anyone her name, not her real one at least, but as a harrowing wind swept through the alley, and the cool hard bricks of the wall behind her penetrated her clothes with their bitterness, she figured she had nothing to lose.

"Agnes Archibald."

"Well, good morrow, Miss Archibald." He tipped his hat. "I am Mr. Watson of Mildred's Court."

Mr. Watson gazed at her with intense blue eyes, and she shifted awkwardly beneath them. He stood a full head taller than her at least and his broad shoulders told her if he wanted to hurt her, he very well could have. But he didn't want to, that much was clear. It seemed he was a gentleman in title and in deed.

He cleared his throat. "Now, are you interested in honest employment or not?"

Her confident façade fell away, and she studied his earnest face for a long moment. "Sir, I don't understand. Why would you offer me employment? I'm a thief."

"You're not a thief, Miss Archibald. You are a woman who steals to survive. There is a difference."

Trembles shuddered through her body as she fought every urge to cave and cry into this saintly man. "Very few people share your opinion, I'm afraid, Mr. Watson. They call me a wretch. A whore. But I swear to you, I ain't never sold myself."

"I'm relieved to hear it, Miss Archibald. I don't believe there is anything so degrading for one of God's children to have to resort to such methods of income. Now, about this employment opportunity—"

But Agnes couldn't answer either way, her mind was so caught on his reference to her. "I'm not a child of God, sir. I'm sorry to say, God has long forgotten me."

A tenderness came like a wave over Mr. Watson's countenance. "Miss Archibald, the fact that I am standing before you today, I believe, is a testament to the fact that He has not."

Chapter 2

Henry Watson led the way through the heart of the grey London morning back to Mildred's Court. From the corner of his eye, he saw Miss Archibald trawling behind him, though she did not utter a single word. When they finally arrived at the gate, his housekeeper Mrs. Green emerged from the house and scolded him like a boy—the way she liked to do as the maternal figure of the household—for not taking the carriage. Anyone might think him a child rather than a man of four-and-twenty, let alone the master of the house.

"For you, Mrs. Green," he said simply and handed her the small bunch of violets.

She softened instantly. "Ah, Mr. Watson, you sweet boy. Now, come, I have a hot pot of tea ready for you."

"Best you fill a hot bath too." He stepped aside to reveal the scrawny woman shivering in his wake on the doorstep.

"Did she follow you here? She ought to be ashamed of herself."

"Mrs. Green, this is Miss—" He turned. "It is *miss*, isn't it?"

"Yes, sir," Miss Archibald replied in a small voice.

"Very good. Mrs. Green, this is Miss Agnes Archibald. She will be assisting you and Charlotte in your work."

"Lottie won't like this one bit."

"Charlotte is upstairs, Miss Archibald shall be downstairs. I doubt they shall ever see one another." He marched directly to his study. "Besides, I'm sure I don't have to remind either of you it is the Christian thing to do to look after this young woman."

"Very well, sir, if you insist." Mrs. Green bundled Miss Archibald down the stairs in the direction of the servant's quarters.

Henry closed the doors on his study, signaling to the staff that he was not to be disturbed, and released a mighty sigh. What was it about that woman that affected him so? He had every right to have her arrested and yet even in retrieving his stolen watch, he could not bring himself to reprimand her in the public eye. There was something about those grey eyes, those masses of chestnut curls that reminded him of a time in his life long forgotten.

He pulled his desk drawer open and rummaged past the pile of papers to the object that had been buried far beneath. The moment his fingers reached the engraved gold case, its cold hard existence struck him to the core. He slowly took the case from its resting place and clicked the tiny button to open it.

There she was. The woman of his nightmares.

Josephine.

The resemblance was uncanny.

Memories he had tried so long to subdue came rising to the surface as he now pondered the look of Miss Archibald—mere skin and bone, dirt-stained face, starved and likely abused.

A cold shiver rippled through him at the thought, and he grounded himself at his desk. The physician had said morning walks would do him good—though he could scarcely claim he was breathing fresh air. But here in his study he knew what to expect and how to conduct his business. Out there was another matter entirely.

Henry became aware of the cold hard facts of the matter. He had allowed his emotions to get in the way. And now of course, he blatantly saw the reason why. The young woman had reminded him so much of—

Hands trembling, he buried the miniature portrait once more and slammed his drawer shut. Henry shook his head and cast away all memories of her. It simply would not do. Agnes Archibald would have to go. What had he been thinking?

Henry waved aside the correspondence that could wait another day for his attention and pulled his Bible from its place on the end table where the tea went cold. The gold-trimmed pages fell open and his stare burned into the words on the page, willing them to speak to his soul. "Guide me, Lord," he prayed from between gritted teeth. "Please Lord, help me to know if it is Your will for that woman to remain in this house, because I fear I acted untrue to myself."

His attention fixed on the words spoken by Jesus Christ himself in his sermon on the mount: *Neither shalt thou swear by thy head, because thou canst not make one hair white or black. But let your communication be Yea, yea; Nay, nay: for whatsoever is more than these cometh from evil.*

He slumped back into the padded velvet chair and scrubbed a hand over his face. Henry had made Agnes Archibald an offer of honest employment and he could not retract it, no matter how impulsively he had behaved, nor how he now dreaded seeing her every day beneath his own roof. It was a cross he had imposed upon himself to bear. Besides, how could he possibly return her to the streets where he'd found her? No, Agnes Archibald would have to stay for her own sake, if not for Henry's standing with God Almighty Himself.

⊰⊱

Agnes couldn't remember the last time she had bathed so thoroughly. Even before she was condemned to the streets of London, Agnes merely waded through the lakes on the borders of her village and figured the watery trek was a sufficient response to the day's chores and grime. But this, she couldn't remember if she'd ever been bathed like this. The room steamed around her flushing her cheeks and floral scents rose from the warm water turning her skin from brown to cream, from callused to soft and wrinkled. Potions anointed her head and the maid Mrs. Green referred to as 'Lottie' was commanded to scrub good and hard, much to the girl's disgust. The maid might have been Agnes' own age, now that she thought about it, but there was such innocence about the doe-eyed lass that Agnes felt at least ten years her senior in life experience.

With every inch of Agnes' skin awake, tingling, and clean, Mrs. Green began to layer the housemaid garb upon her body, finishing with the most elegant raven dress trimmed with white lace and a matching laced apron. It took Mrs. Green, Lottie, and even the round and vivacious cook Miss Kingsley, to tame Agnes' hair. Much of it fell to the floor in clumps but in all Agnes' faults and misgivings of ladylikeness, her hair was her one saving grace. She had her papa's curls and her mam's plenty, so the knotted tresses on the floor would scarcely be missed. It was still rather dull from lack of nourishment but now that it no longer crawled with lice, there was—dare she suggest—a slight prettiness to it. Even Lottie would have had to admit it, were it not for her sour silence. Miss Kingsley, however, was not so particular and self-effacing.

"My my, you do scrub up well," she bellowed and laughed heartily to herself. "Who would have thought. It seems a pity to cover it with a cap."

"But cover it, we shall, Miss Kingsley," Mrs. Green said and used brute force to tame Agnes' curls and pin them upon her head before smothering them with a maid's cap. Even then, stray curls peeked out disobediently despite Mrs. Green's best efforts. "Well, you best be careful with that unruly hair of yours, Miss Archibald. Hen—Mr. Watson—won't want to find it in his breakfast."

"No, of course not. I shall be careful." Agnes meant her promise. She would be careful in every sense of the word if it meant she got warm clothes and a roof over her head.

"Now, let's get you fed, Miss Archibald, else you'll waste away before we even put you to work." Miss Kingsley led her upstairs toward the kitchen and Agnes was careful not to trip on the leather boots that were two full sizes too big. "Don't worry, Mrs. Green will sort you out. Not none of us have as small a foot as you, you see. And well, it's not like Mr. Watson gave us much notice of your coming."

Agnes glanced up and almost lost her footing on the last carpeted stair. "No, of course, not. I am grateful you had anything remotely my size."

"Well, that dress there belonged to young Lottie before she started eating my raspberry tarts. Give me time, Miss Archibald, and I'll fatten you up too."

Agnes smiled to herself. She was looking forward to it.

Miss Kingsley swung the door open, revealing an immense room with countless cupboards, a sizable larder, and an intimidating black stove in the far corner. An inconspicuous door stood in the opposite corner. "That'd be your room, miss. Just through there. It hasn't been used in some time, but we keep the sheets fresh, and everything dusted, as is the way. Mr. Watson is very particular about things being clean."

"May I?" she asked in a small voice.

"Of course, tis your room now, Miss Archibald. You help yourself in there while I fetch you some salted porridge."

The door creaked beneath Agnes' touch. A light-filled room greeted her, the wide window overlooking a vegetable patch. A pristine cream quilt with blue rose buds dressed the white-iron bed, a washstand stood in the corner with a lady and gentleman painted upon the jug and basin, and a dresser with coiled legs and a looking glass stood at the far end of the bedroom. It may have been small by another's standards, but Miss Kingsley's words filled her heart with hope. This was her room now. Hers. Nothing had been truly hers except for the tattered flea-infested clothes from her back. But as she peered into the looking glass now, she no longer recognized the Agnes Archibald of the streets. Before her was a presentable housemaid on the cusp of eating a hearty warm meal.

Perhaps God had not forgotten her after all.

Chapter 3

Agnes' stubborn determination to survive translated well into tenacious efficiency in her work. She barely saw Mr. Watson during the work day, unless Mrs. Green was otherwise engaged and so Agnes had to deliver a tea tray to him in his study.

The first time it came crashing to the floor.

She foolishly nudged her way through the doors only to have them swing back and shatter all her efforts to be the quiet and respectful downstairs maid she was desperately trying to be. She opened her mouth only to further condemn herself, cursing beneath her breath as she gathered up the fine bone China. Mr. Watson—gentleman he was—met her on the ground to assist her.

"Please don't. It's my fault, sir, I should have been more careful." Agnes gently pushed his hands away from the mess, but anyone might have thought she'd bitten him the way he recoiled from her. She supposed he thought her still tainted from life on the streets. Then again, the way he looked at her, even standing back to observe her, she simply could not work him out.

When she rose to her full height, even if she was short in stature, Agnes lifted her chin and met that same iron stare she had seen in the back alley. "Forgive me for the commotion, it won't happen again, sir. I'll be sure to be more careful in future. And please take the damage out of my wages, sir."

"Miss Archibald. It is only a teacup."

Her strong resolve dissipated beneath what she could only read as a look of compassion. Perhaps, Mr. Watson wasn't as hard as iron as he seemed, not as cool and aloof as she had first presumed.

He straightened. "But if you don't mind, I should like another cup."

"Of course, sir."

Agnes never spilled the tea again. She quickly learned to push the door open with her backside and ease her way into the room as quiet as a thief. Or rather, as quiet as a downstairs maid ought to be. She did so want to impress him. Perhaps, a little too much.

Every day before sunrise, Agnes eagerly filled the buckets with thirty pounds of coal for the fires before boiling water for Lottie to take upstairs. Agnes had offered to help her once—only once—for the disgusted look she received from the upstairs maid at the very suggestion kept Agnes firmly in her stationed place. Miss Kingsley, however, frequently took her up on her offer of help and trusted her to assist in preparing the meals for the day. Sometimes Agnes would even be trusted to serve Mr. Watson in the breakfast room, gently placing the tray with its domed silver lid before him on the starched white linen cloth as though she were born for the task. Often, he had salted porridge, which he would thank the Lord for before eating. But on other mornings he would have eggs and potted beef with buttery toast, and this brought a smile out of Mr. Watson and his prayer of thanks held a little more joy. Such a breakfast brought a smile out of Agnes too when she got to eat the plentiful helpings leftover from Miss Kingsley's generous kitchen. Once Agnes' morning chores were complete and her hands stung from scrubbing the pots in scalding water, she'd sit by the hearth in the kitchen and relish in one of the three guaranteed meals for the day before the afternoon chores demanded her zealous attention.

One particularly grey afternoon, when Mr. Watson took tea in his study, his voice stopped her mid-step before she could return to her work.

"How are you enjoying your employment, Miss Archibald?"

She turned and met the stare she was becoming so fond of. "I like it very much, Mr. Watson. How could I not?"

"And everyone treats you well?"

"Almost everyone, yes." It had been her instinctual response but the moment the words left her mouth, she regretted them. "I mean, yes, of course, everyone treats me very well, sir."

"Is it Charlotte? Has she said something to you?" He cleared his throat. "I understand she has been known to be rather difficult."

"Well, it's not so much what she has said but what she hasn't said, I suppose."

"Go on."

Agnes stepped toward the desk acting as a clear partition between his station and her own. "She has never actually spoken a word to me."

"Never?"

"No, not one, though I'd sooner prefer that than to know what's going through her mind."

His lips twitched into a half-smile. "You must understand, she is Mrs. Green's niece, and were that dear woman not so faithful to the Watson family, I assure you Charlotte would have no place here."

"I see."

He arched a brow. "I hope I can trust you with that sort of information, Miss Archibald. I understand it could be tempting to use it to your advantage."

"I've never had anyone trust me with much, Mr. Watson. Probably, for good reason. But I've never had anyone believe in me either. Till you." Agnes watched as a cloud passed over his face till there appeared a mixture of wonder and pain. "So, excuse me for being so bold, sir, but I will be loyal to you forever."

Her statement was followed by silence, so she attempted a makeshift curtsey—as she'd seen the pristine Lottie do a thousand times before—then escaped with hot cheeks to her room. And there, in the privacy of a place she could finally call her own, Agnes Archibald cried.

"Foolish girl, why are you crying?" she scolded herself and glared into the mirror. "You may clean up, but you'll always be a street wretch. You're not worthy to kiss the ground he walks on, let alone—"

Her head fell upon her folded arms, and she released the heavy sobs she'd been holding in for the past three years since her parents' deaths. It seemed grace had finally broken her in.

❧

With his attention seized by the space Agnes Archibald's presence had left, Henry's jaw slackened, and his mind raced. He had tried to remain distant with the girl but when she looked at him with those eyes of hers, he feared it was within her power to undo him completely. He hadn't meant to strike up conversation with her, but once again his mouth had run away from him. Much like it had done that morning when Agnes Archibald catapulted into his life.

When the door swung open a moment later, so fixated was he upon it that he flinched in his chair and jolted to sit upright.

"What on earth have you done to poor Miss Archibald?" Mrs. Green asked, closing the door behind herself.

"She was positively fine a moment ago."

"Hmm." Mrs. Green's mouth twisted in consideration.

"Perhaps she doesn't feel at home here after all," he wondered aloud. "Does she have everything she needs, Mrs. Green?"

"Of course, sir. She has many of Lottie's old things."

"She has been here some weeks now, perhaps you could organize to purchase some things of her own? Something suitable so she can attend church gatherings with the servants."

Mrs. Green lowered her voice. "Mr. Watson, I don't want to shock you, but I don't believe she shares our faith in Christ."

"Maybe she hasn't been given the chance." Henry felt his neck flush and was grateful for his high stiff collar. Surely, he didn't have to defend his reasonings to buy the young woman a Sunday dress. In an attempt at distraction, he began to sort through the documents he had been preparing for his upcoming trip to Bath.

"You know, sir, it has not escaped me," she began carefully, "the resemblance—"

Henry took his quill and squeezed it in his fingertips. "I cannot pretend to know what you're referring to, Mrs. Green."

"Very well, sir." She sighed. "You know we are all very fond of Miss Archibald, and she certainly is a good worker, but—"

He peered up at her. "Only "good"?"

"Well, you know her, sir. She is eager, I will give her that."

"Yes, if only everyone shared her work ethic."

Mrs. Green fluttered a hand to her chest. "Sir?"

"All I mean to say, Mrs. Green, is that she is most grateful to be here, and I would like her to feel at home and welcome in this place. Does that seem like such an abhorrent request to you?"

"No, no of course not."

"Then I should like you to see to this matter, if you would be so kind. Just be sure to tell Charlotte she'll be responsible to assist Miss Kingsley today and be responsible for both upstairs and down—for I understand she thinks Agnes' efforts redundant at best anyway."

Mrs. Green looked positively aghast but swallowed her opinions and withdrew with a small, "Yes, sir."

Finally alone, Henry Watson smirked to himself and gazed out at the grey day. Perhaps Agnes Archibald was not a burden after all. Perhaps, she had been just what he needed.

Chapter 4

From the haberdasheries to the milliners to the drapers and dressmakers, Agnes obediently followed as Mrs. Green shuffled down Oxford Street and practiced the well-learned art of shopping. Agnes remained silent for many of the decisions, simply nodding when Mrs. Green insisted she needed a certain item—gloves, stockings, a bonnet for church, another hat for the outdoors, and one good dress for Sunday or a rare afternoon free from chores.

"We will go with the blue, I think." The dressmaker adjusted the spectacles on her long nose and fingered the fabrics Mrs. Green had selected at the drapers. "Blue is most definitely her color. I shall have a dress delivered to Mr. Watson's residence by Friday."

Agnes glanced up from a myriad of rainbow ribbons, excited it could all come to pass so soon.

"Then perhaps you might like to wear one to church come Sunday," Mrs. Green suggested with a sideways glance.

"I would be happy to attend if I have something suitable to wear," Agnes said swiftly.

The dressmaker circled her like a vulture. "Suitable? By the time I'm done with you, you'll be fit to visit Westminster Abbey."

On their way back to the carriage, Agnes tried to keep up with Mrs. Green, hitching her skirt a little to avoid the piles of manure and sludge on the cobblestone street. "I've never had lovely things. Not even back in the country. Papa was a farmer, you see, so I was used to hard work. I had one decent dress for Sunday but even then it would get soiled. I do hope I shan't do anything to ruin these clothes. Not after—"

"Miss Archibald, they will be your things to do with as you please."

Mrs. Green paused at the carriage, and the footman eagerly climbed down from his post. He offered his hand, and she grunted in appreciation as he assisted her into the carriage. Before he could offer the same courtesy to

Agnes, she clambered inside on her own, causing a hint of a smile to dance upon his mouth.

❧

Upon returning to the house, Agnes removed the hand-me-down bonnet and cloak and withdrew to her own private part of the house. She managed to forget herself for a moment and wistfully fell back into the plush quilts upon the bed. Hand to her heart, she wondered over the happenings of the day. Never had she been the receiver of such consideration, and if Mrs. Green had taken her to town on that very particular mission, then she knew she must have sought Mr. Watson's permission to do so. Not to mention, it had to have been his money funding the purchases. How could she ever repay Mr. Watson for such kindness and generosity?

Her bedroom door snapped shut, jolting her out of her daydream and forcing her upright. Lottie leaned against the door, arms folded, disdain tainting her face.

"Did you have a pleasant afternoon?"

Agnes swallowed hard. If Lottie meant to frighten her, she was testing the wrong woman. "What do you want, Lottie?"

"It's Miss Green to you."

"Forgive me for the lack of formality. Believe me, I don't intend to be on personal terms with you anymore than I believe you do with me."

She arched her brow. "Oh, we are high and mighty today, aren't we?"

Agnes rose from the bed and straightened her dress. "This is my private room. You are trespassing."

"I'm sure you know all about that. All about broken rules. Broken laws. See, I know where you came from, Agnes Archibald, and you'll be back in the gutter soon enough when Henry tires of you."

It was the first time Agnes had heard someone use his Christian name.

"Soon, you too will be replaced by someone younger and prettier than you."

Agnes smirked. "You think I'm prettier than you?"

"That's not what I—"

"Lottie, please leave before I throw you out. Do not underestimate me. I can and I will."

Her mouth gaped and she struggled to counter with a response. She gripped the handle till her fingers drained white and flung the door open. "So help me, I will ruin you, Agnes Archibald."

"Get out."

The door crashed beneath Lottie's frustration, and once she was alone Agnes allowed her tears to fall. Twice in one day she had cried, what on earth was the matter with her?

Heavy footfalls approached and she swiped beneath her eyes just in time for Mr. Watson to burst into the room.

"What is going on—" His broad stature melted before her. "Agnes? Whatever is the matter?"

"Nothing at all, sir. I'm just so grateful, sir."

"So grateful you go about slamming doors? I was looking for Mrs. Green and heard a raucous."

She hung her head. "Lottie was here. Please don't say anything, it'll just make things worse."

"Agnes, look at me."

She did as she was bid. Agnes had thought his eyes to be blue, but it seemed they had flecks of green, like the ocean on a summer day.

"I want you to remember something. It's very important. Are you listening?"

"Yes, sir."

A struggle swept over his countenance and for the briefest moment she wondered what it would be like to call him by his Christian name, like he had suddenly taken to using hers.

"I believe God brought you here for a purpose, even if you cannot see it now. In the Kingdom of God, station does not matter. There is no rich and poor, not in the sense that we understand. As a child of God, you have every right to know Him, no matter what anyone else says. Do you understand?"

"No," she whispered in earnest, "but I so desperately want to."

"Then, Agnes Archibald, I shall pray that you will."

Chapter 5

Before the sun rose over the bleak December day, Agnes completed her morning chores, and readied herself for church. It took both Mrs. Green and Miss Kingsley to help her into her pale blue muslin dress and matching bonnet. She had never known so many layers to be required for dressing, so many in fact she felt like one of Miss Kingsley's pastries. Still, for the first time in her young life, she emerged from her private room feeling every bit the lady, and never more so when Henry Watson stopped short in his strides toward the front door to glance in her direction. A thousand fireflies set off in every direction within Agnes' middle, and she tried to ignore Lottie's incredulous stare.

The Sunday morning gathering was less intimidating than Agnes first expected, and she listened to the speakers with a combination of wonder and confusion. But it was not until the hall erupted in song that Agnes had to fight rising emotions. A strange feeling swelled in her chest, sending gooseflesh down her arms, as the people in the house of God lifted their voices in the final verse. *"Finish, then, Thy new creation; true and spotless let us be. Let us see Thy great salvation perfectly restored in thee. Changed from glory into glory, till in heav'n we take our place, till we cast our crowns before thee, lost in wonder, love and praise."*

The word 'spotless' evoked something in her. Her eyes misted. How she longed to be true and spotless, and yet how she feared she never would be.

Agnes had been placed beside Miss Kingsley for the service, so when the formalities concluded, Miss Kingsley subtly advised her of the upper crust individuals who were particular friends of Mr. Watson. "And that over there is Mr. and Mrs. Fry," she said in undertones, "they will be attending Mr. Watson's much anticipated Christmas dinner."

Agnes met her quiet tone while bobbing a polite curtsey to the fellow servants who passed them by in the back pews. "Is there to be a dinner party, Miss Kingsley?"

"Yes, indeed. This coming Friday night."

"But what shall I wear then? I wore my best dress today."

Miss Kingsley chuckled. "Oh, don't fret, dear. You'll just be wearing your uniform like the rest of us."

"Of course, how silly of me."

Agnes swiftly recovered, shaking her head. What was she thinking? Of course she would be serving for the Christmas dinner. In her heart, she secretly blamed Henry Watson's kindness for her even contemplating such a ridiculous thought. Agnes had to remind herself that despite any feelings she might have, there was a line she could never cross. She would forever be of the working class, and she ought to be grateful for it. She was now a downstairs maid, which was certainly an elevation from what she had been as a thief on the streets of London. She had been no better than vermin. And Henry Watson, well, he was the master of the house, and a man who deserved so much more than a broken woman would ever be able to give.

That afternoon Agnes delivered the tea tray to Mr. Watson's study, only he was nowhere to be found. She rested the tray on the end table and was about to withdraw directly when she noticed some books piled on a nearby chair. It was the only part of the handsome room out of place and remembering his desire for all things tidy and clean, Agnes set to put them away in the bookcase. The bookcase was organized alphabetically so she would have little trouble finding the appropriate places. Only when she picked up the heavy book from the top of the pile and realized it was a copy of God's very own word, did she still. Her fingers trailed the spine then recoiled for fear of tainting it.

"It won't bite," Mr. Watson said from the open doorway.

"Oh, it's not that." She swiftly returned the great book to its place. "I just don't want to go spoiling its pages." She dipped into a curtsey. "Forgive me, sir, I was only going to put them away. But I found myself—"

"Distracted?"

"Exactly, sir."

"The word of God has a habit of doing that." He closed the space between them and reached to pick up the book.

"I was just bringing the tea," Agnes went on, "and noticed these out of place, I just wanted it true and spotless in here for you."

Henry paused, hands tight around his Bible. "True and spotless?"

"Yes, sir. Excuse me, sir."

But Watson's curiosity visibly piqued. "Tell me, what did you think of the church gathering this morning?"

"Confusing," she admitted, "yet wonderful."

"*Love Divine All Things Excelling*, that was the song."

She looked up to meet his eye.

"The song you quoted just now."

Agnes felt the warmth rise to her cheeks, but she couldn't bring herself to look away from him. Not when she felt so seen. "Do you truly believe people can be true and spotless," she asked softly then added a small, "sir?"

"Of course, I believe it, that is why Jesus Christ died on the cross, after all."

"I see."

"Tell me, can you read?"

"Yes, sir. My mam made sure of it."

"Then I have something for you." He eased his way past her toward the bookcase and pulled out a small leather-bound book. "Here is the Bible I used as a boy. You can read it, if you want. Perhaps start with the book of Romans."

"Romans?"

"Yes, let me mark it for you." He opened his desk drawer and pulled out a white ribbon. He then found the place in the book with a few turns of the page, laid the ribbon within, and handed it to her.

Agnes' fingers wrapped around it, and she pressed it to her chest. She fought the rising tears with every ounce of strength. "Thank you," she breathed.

"Agnes? Are you alright?"

She nodded, but she herself could feel the sting in her eyes willing to escape. "Yes, of course. This is wonderful, sir. I will take good care of it, of course, and give it back to you."

"So long as you are in this house, Agnes, it is yours. Do you understand?"

The first tear escaped without permission, and she reached to smooth it away. "I am sorry, sir."

"Won't you sit down? Take a moment?"

She shook her head. "No, thank you, sir. I should get back to work."

"Of course. Well, here." He reached into his pocket and pulled out a handkerchief with the letters "H.W." embroidered upon it.

Cradling the small Bible with one arm, she reached for the handkerchief and pressed it to her damp face. It smelled of musk with a hint of lavender. Most of the drawers in the house had a sprig of lavender within.

"Thank you, sir," she whispered.

He gazed at her for a long moment. "Is there something I can do for you?"

"No, thank you, sir. I have stayed long enough." She sniffed. "I should return to—"

"You do know I am the one who pays your wages."

She stifled a laugh. "Are you telling me you are willing to pay me to just stand here and cry?"

"Well, I would not use those exact terms. But I should like to see you happy and well."

"These are happy tears, sir. I assure you. First with the dress, and now this..."

"You like the dress then?"

"It is the most beautiful thing I have ever owned, and I haven't had a chance to even thank you."

He leaned forward, mirth dancing in his eyes. "Well, now's your chance."

"Thank you," she said swiftly, pressing the handkerchief to her eyes.

He straightened and a smile impressed upon his handsome face. "You are most welcome, Agnes."

She innocently held the handkerchief toward him.

He chuckled. "You can keep that too."

"I fear you're going to become sick of me thanking you, sir." She bowed her head, glancing down at the book within her hands, then turned to withdraw.

"Thank you for the tea."

Agnes paused at the door and peered over her shoulder at Henry Watson who stood unmoved. "It's the least I can do, sir." She bit her lip and slipped away, clasping the Bible to her chest.

Chapter 6

Henry sipped his tea and stared out at the rain pelting against the window, lost in thought. His chest felt tight as he recalled the way Agnes had clung to that Bible, the way her eyes glistened with gratitude.

"True and spotless," he whispered the prayer of his heart to the very ears of God.

When the dinner gong rang out, Henry stirred from his desk, not realizing the time nor the darkness of the room. He quietly made his way to the dining room, fully expecting Mrs. Green to be waiting with another of Miss Kingsley's hearty meals. Only, it wasn't Mrs. Green waiting for him in the dining hall, but Agnes.

She dipped into a curtsey. "Mrs. Green has a headache, sir. So, I will be serving dinner, if that is all right with you, sir."

"Of course."

Henry took his seat at the head of the table and watched Agnes remove the domed lid before pacing the distance to the buffet where other small dishes lay. Then she stood with her back toward the buffet, head bowed, eyes closed. Waiting.

Henry cleared his throat and bowed his head. "Father in heaven, thank You for our daily bread. Please bless it to our bodies, and please help Agnes better understand You as she reads Your Word. In the name of Jesus I pray, Amen." He glanced up to find Agnes frozen against the buffet. "Is everything all right?"

"Yes, of course." She straightened, seemingly coming out of a trance, and reached for the first dish. Silently, she made her way toward him, offering a selection of vegetables.

He nodded. "Please."

She slowly ladled them onto his plate.

Henry watched her work, wishing their situations were different. How he longed to have her sit beside him and share in the meal and continue their discussion from earlier that day.

"Beg your pardon, sir, but is that sufficient?"

He glanced down at his plate to see it loaded with green. He raised his hand. "Yes, yes, my apologies. I should have told you so three spoonsful ago. But I was somewhat—"

"Distracted?"

"Yes, quite."

She silently returned the dish to the buffet.

"Is anything the matter?" he asked. "You seem as preoccupied as myself."

She spun to face him. "What does it mean when it says there is no condemnation for those who are in Christ Jesus? Surely, there are still consequences for our mistakes."

Henry settled back in his chair and tried not to smile. "Ah, chapter eight."

"Yes, and what does it mean to walk with the Spirit?"

He cleared his throat. "Well, in regard to your first question, there may always be worldly consequences for our mistakes but once we accept that Jesus Christ died for our sins and desire Him as Lord over our lives, then we are not condemned in the eyes of God, and we have eternity to look forward to with Him."

She nodded slowly, reached for the wine, and poured it into his glass. She lingered so close, he almost forgot once again to raise his hand but did so before the glass overfilled and spilt all over the tablecloth. "And what of the other?"

He cleansed his dry throat with the wine and silently prayed he would do the answer justice. "When Jesus ascended to heaven once again, He promised to send a comforter, the Spirit of God for the children of God. When one accepts Christ, they accept the comforter as well. The Spirit begins to move in their life and guide them. Albeit silently. Well, at least as far as we mortals understand." He shook his head. "I am not explaining this very well."

Agnes lingered beside him, holding the decanter with both hands, a faraway look in her eyes.

He peered up at her, she was standing far too close for his comfort. He felt that familiar flush rise up his neck, warming his face. "Was there something else?"

"No, thank you, sir, that was all for now," she said softly and returned to stand by the buffet.

He finally picked up his knife and fork.

"Actually, since you ask," she began again, curiosity written on her face. "How does one begin?"

"Begin?"

Her gaze fell. "Yes, you know, to believe. How does one begin?"

He swallowed the lump in his throat. Suddenly, he wasn't hungry anymore. He rested his cutlery beside his plate. "One prays, Agnes," he began softly. "One asks the Lord Jesus Christ to forgive them and to be Lord of their lives."

"Is that all?"

"Yes," he breathed, fighting his own emotions. He grasped his trembling hands together and laid them in his lap. What was the matter with him? Why did this woman bring out such feelings in him?

"Thank you, sir," she said softly.

He attempted not to cringe over the title she used so often. How he wished he could just be *Henry*. Not 'Mr. Watson'. Not 'sir'. To be just a young man speaking to a young woman like his equal. And not in such a delicate situation either, where he knew there were clear lines he could not cross. Would not cross. Really should not cross.

Lost in confusion and wonder, Agnes considered whether the prayer had to be spoken aloud or if she could pray it in this moment, in the depths of her heart. How she wanted to be true and spotless. How she wished the shame and guilt that hung over her head for every item pilfered and sold, over every home she had looted under the cover of darkness, over every malice intention and every corrupt thought. If Henry only understood how terrible she had been, he wouldn't be offering her a life free of condemnation. He wouldn't have even offered her a position beneath his roof.

"May I enquire after your thoughts?" he asked.

"Might I be excused, sir? If there is nothing else you require?"

"No, nothing at all."

She curtseyed and swiftly withdrew, leaving behind a somewhat bewildered Henry Watson. She raced to the privacy of her room, politely refusing the offer of dinner from Miss Kingsley as she passed through the kitchen.

Closing the door behind her, she dropped to her knees and finally released the flood of tears she had been holding in.

"Lord Jesus," she sobbed. "I am filth. I am worthless. But I don't want to be. Please, please forgive me. Forgive me for it all." She pressed her forehead to the pages of God's Word still open on her bed. "Forgive me. Please, make me true and spotless."

Agnes slept sound that night for the first time in a long time, despite her empty stomach. However, with the morning came the harshness of reality.

While Agnes stoked the stove's fire for Miss Kingsley, a voice interrupted her thoughts still lingering on her prayer the evening before.

"What's this?" Lottie asked, holding up Henry's childhood Bible.

Agnes flinched. "What were you doing in my room?"

"This says it belongs to Henry," she sneered. "Did you steal it?"

"No. He gave it to me. Now give it back."

Lottie's countenance visibly shifted from shock to genuine fury. "He gave this to you? Why?"

Agnes folded her arms across her chest. "I had questions after the gathering, that is all. He thought—"

"Questions? You?" she spat. "Agnes Archibald, for all the crimes you have committed, the devil has reserved a place in hell for you already!"

Agnes' heart thumped in her chest as she watched Lottie circle her like a bird of prey. "That's not true. It says there is now no condemnation for those who are in Christ Jesus."

A mist covered Lottie's eyes and she gritted her teeth. "How could Jesus forgive all you've done? And are still doing. There's no doubt you stole this. You're just lying."

"Ask Henry yourself."

Her eyebrows leapt and instantly Agnes regretted using his Christian name. "Oh, it's Henry now, is it? In any case, I can't. He's gone."

"Gone? Gone where?"

"Didn't he tell you? Well, I suppose you must not be so special after all."

Agnes braced herself. "Regardless, give back that Bible."

Lottie grinned. "If you want it, fetch."

Before Agnes could reach for the precious copy gifted from Henry Watson's own hand, Lottie threw it into the open stove. Instantly, the leather charred, and the pages coiled and blackened. "No!"

"And that is the fate that awaits you also," Lottie said simply.

Miss Kingsley burst into the kitchen with arms full of produce. "What is going on in here? I could hear you two from the front door."

Lottie looked at Agnes expectantly, but Agnes simply pressed her lips together and determined she was not going to give Lottie the satisfaction of seeing her cry.

"Nothing," Agnes stammered and escaped while she still had the self-control to do so. "Nothing at all."

Chapter 7

Business had forced Henry Watson to Bath early that week, though he could scarcely concentrate on the task at hand. Mrs. Green had assured him she would look after Agnes in his stead, but he doubted if it came to it that she would defend the young woman against her own niece. He therefore enlisted the help of Miss Kingsley as well, who knew just what Charlotte Green could be like.

In an attempt to shorten his stay, Henry rejected every social invitation he received during his time in Bath. He only met with the fellow investors when he was prevailed upon to do so but otherwise finalized the documents required in the privacy of his rooms. As soon as he could excuse himself, he quitted Bath society and returned to the stale soot of London where he knew the company would be more to his taste. However, upon his return, he was surprised to discover that Agnes didn't seem pleased to see him in the least. Or if she was, she hid it unmistakably well.

"Did everyone treat you well while I was away?"

He watched her place the tea tray down on the end table and waited for her to look up at him, but she did not.

Agnes bowed her head and bobbed a small curtsey. "Yes, sir."

"Agnes?"

"Yes, sir."

"I am glad you seem to be so fond of your new boots, but do you suppose you might look at me?"

Those grey eyes peered up from beneath full lashes. He swore she was becoming prettier by the day now that she had nourishing meals and a home to call her own.

"There you are."

She shook her head. "Mr. Watson, you can't keep doing this."

"What, travel? I promise, I only have to go a few times a year. You see, some gentlemen I do business with frequent there and—"

"No *this*." Tears pricked her eyes and he saw her battle against them. "Whatever this is." She gestured between the two of them. "It can't go on."

He intentionally rounded the desk to close the space between them. "Agnes—"

"I am Miss Archibald, the downstairs maid. You are Henry Watson, the master of the house. You cannot favor me, sir. God only knows, I don't deserve it."

"I do believe that's the first time you have said my name."

She shook her head again, stepping away. "Please, sir. Do not give me false hopes and misplaced attention."

Fire sparked in his core, and he pursued her across the room. "Was it not you who said you would be loyal to me forever? How is it you are permitted to speak your heart, but I am not?"

"I'm not worthy to hear what it has to say," she snapped.

Henry saw a glimpse of that woman he had seen in the alley all those weeks ago. Only this time he knew that the same defensiveness and self-degradation she displayed simply masked her true feelings—she was terrified. She had been afraid that morning when he'd caught her in the act of stealing, and she was afraid now at the idea of him seeing more in her than what she thought she was condemned to be.

He exhaled loudly and kept his voice steady and calm. "Because you are a maid?"

"Because I am filth. All the pretty dresses in the world can't change that, Mr. Watson."

He shook his head. "What did Charlotte say to you while I was away? I demand you tell me."

"Nothing I didn't already know."

"Oh, blast it." Henry closed the space between them. "Miss Archibald, would you please allow me to confess my true—"

Mrs. Green gasped as she stood in the open doorway, forcing them both to look up. It was then he realized, he had taken Agnes' hands in his own and now, rather than pulling away, she clasped his tighter.

Mrs. Green's hand flew to her mouth. "Henry! What is the meaning of this?"

❧

As the shock of the moment faded, Agnes forced herself away from Henry Watson faster than a hare in hunting season.

"Henry, what is the matter with you?" Mrs. Green demanded.

"Mrs. Green, I am not a child."

"But she might as well be! Honestly, sir." Mrs. Green shook her head and reached for Agnes. "Come on now, Miss Archibald, I expected more from you—"

"Do not forget your place, Mrs. Green," Henry said, his voice rising for the first time in Agnes' memory. "I am the master of the house, not some boy beneath your instruction."

"Then act like it," she quipped, "and leave this poor girl alone. Now, Agnes, come!" Mrs. Green marched toward the study doors. Agnes proceeded to follow.

"Agnes, please stay."

Just his voice in her direction would have been enough to halt her completely, but she could never ignore the gentle request in it.

Mrs. Green shot a vicious glare over her shoulder. "Mr. Watson, she is not Josephine. No matter what you do for this girl, you cannot change the past."

Agnes searched his face. "What is she talking about?"

"Take the afternoon off, Mrs. Green, for you are clearly perplexed," Henry said. "I hope to see you at your work tomorrow much improved. Please, do close the door on your way out."

"Suit yourselves, but you are fools if you believe anything can come from this!"

Agnes winced as the door thundered closed—now she knew where the niece inherited her temper.

"Forgive me," Henry said softly, "I shouldn't have taken advantage of my position like that."

Her brows knitted together. "With Mrs. Green?"

"And with you, I suppose." Henry leaned back against the desk with a deep sigh. "I don't want you to think this is a habit of mine. I have never crossed a line with a member of staff before." He then quietly added, "I am not my father."

Agnes swallowed hard. "Then who was Miss Josephine?"

"Agnes, I think it best we sit down."

"Did you forget who you're speaking to? I'm not easily shocked, sir."

"I simply meant it is a rather long tale." He gestured to the pair of olive-green velvet armchairs by the bookcase. "Won't you sit down with me? Please?"

Agnes didn't want to dirty his furniture with her well-worked uniform. Still, she followed him over to the chairs as he asked. She dared not admit she would follow that man anywhere should he ask her.

He cleared his throat and leaned forward in the chair. "Miss Josephine was my father's ward. She was a few years older than me, but I fancied myself quite in love with her. Mind, I was only twelve."

A smile touched Agnes' lips. "Go on."

"Well, one day she disappeared. I was concerned, though no one else seemed to be. So, I had it in my mind that I was going to find her and rescue her."

"And did you find her?"

"I asked around, paid for information, that sort of thing. One time I was even mugged by a gang, but yes, eventually, I found her."

"And?"

"She was servicing a client at the back of a hotel in broad daylight."

Agnes swallowed the information like a mouthful of bile, knowing all too well that that might have been her had she allowed herself to endure it. "I'm sorry."

"So was I."

"She didn't just disappear, did she?"

"No, as it turns out she ran away. I discovered from her own mouth—rather aggressively, I might add—that my father had been abusing her for years, and she would rather have given herself away on her own terms."

"I can't even imagine how that must have affected you."

"I thought my father a Christian man, Agnes, but he was a hypocrite. I saw far too much that day that a young man ought not to see. It was after that day that the nightmares began."

She shifted in the chair to better face him. "How did you get them to stop?"

"The nightmares? I didn't." He shrugged. "Couldn't, I suppose. I don't have them so often now, but I must admit after our first encounter, they started again."

"This all explains a great deal."

"It helped when I learned that there were true Christians in the world professing Christ with their lives and not through mere words. The gatherings help me immensely, as does praying, and being in the Word, of course."

"Well, thank you for telling me." Agnes slowly began to stand but one touch from his hand stilled her.

"I know you're not her, Agnes. You may have reminded me of her at the beginning, but I believe that is why the Lord allowed our paths to cross."

"He knew no one else would take pity on me."

"No, Agnes. He knew that I would be bound to believe in you, and to extend His grace to you, because He loves you."

His final words to her weighed heavy in the air between them and she couldn't help but wonder if there was a double meaning behind them. Or rather, she permitted herself to hope.

∍

"Lord, please help me to do what is right," Henry whispered as he pored over the pages of God's Word the following morning. With the blood-red ribbon still lingering in the Gospel of Matthew, he went onto read chapter 25. Once again, the words of his Lord and Savior Jesus Christ rose from the page and struck his heart. *And the King shall answer and say unto them, Verily I say unto you, Inasmuch as ye have done it unto one of the least of these my brethren, ye have done it unto me.*

Henry knew what needed to be done, but executing his plan required a delicacy he was not sure he possessed. Still, there was no possible way Agnes could serve at the dinner party, not if he were to let his intentions be known to Agnes and if she was to accept him. And as much as he believed his guests were true Christians and would not judge her, it would be the transition of moving her from server to being served that would cause the most disturbance. No, if he was to act, then it had to be today, before the guests arrived for dinner. With so much to do in preparation to ready the house, he knew Agnes' day would be filled with endless chores, but if he could just have a few moments with her again, he could assure her of his honest affections. Of course, he had single ladies of his acquaintance who others might deem a more appropriate match, but none of them had challenged him the way Agnes did. Her very survival and diligent work since entering honest employment, challenged him in ways he never thought possible. He had always lived a comfortable life, and never considered the strength it would take to survive day-to-day and apply oneself so heartily for the sake of bettering one's position as well as selflessly helping others. Yes, there may be many young ladies in London, but there was only one Agnes Archibald. And after the happenings of yesterday, he was not about to allow Charlotte or Mrs. Green to bully Agnes out of this house. No, he was not.

Chapter 8

The first glimpse of Christmas arrived at Mildred's Court on Friday morning. Mrs. Green hung evergreen boughs over the doorway before twisting them up the staircase rail, while Miss Kingsley prepared the goose and the brandy pudding. Lottie cleaned chamber pots and Agnes scrubbed the thick dining hall rug four inches at a time. She was certain the house would be beautiful— enchanted, even—by the time the dinner guests arrived. How she wished she could be one of them instead of preparing the ground for them to spill their drinks upon.

Agnes smoothed stray curls from her forehead and grasped the brush with both hands. Back and forth she went with a vivacity that only testified to her frustration. She'd likely be here all morning but so long as Henry didn't enter, she could accept being a sweating mess. When his voice echoed from the adjoining hallway, she startled and leapt upright, straightening her skirts, and smoothing her hair back beneath her maid's cap.

Agnes waited for Henry's voice to draw near, for the door to swing open and for him to be in search of her. That was until an authoritative voice rose above Henry's distant pleasantries.

"We received word from Mrs. Green that several silver spoons are missing. She sent for us to come and investigate."

"If this is true, then I should prefer to investigate myself," Henry responded, meeting the officer's tone in both volume and candor.

"This is a matter for the police now, Mr. Watson. It would be disrespectful to the Crown not to follow through on such a matter."

"Constable—"

Agnes' heart thrashed in her chest and her head suddenly felt light. She was innocent. She knew she was innocent. So why did she feel so guilty?

Agnes emerged from the dining hall with flushed cheeks. "What's going on?"

"Please remain in the hallway while we search the premises, miss," the constable ordered brusquely before marching downstairs.

Henry paused long enough to watch the constable disappear down the stairs, then looked over his shoulder at Agnes. He gently raised his hand as though to calm her racing heart. "It's all right, Agnes. I am sure it's just a misunderstanding." Then Henry, too, disappeared from sight.

Mrs. Green, Miss Kingsley, and Lottie were all sent to the hallway to await the verdict that was to come. Agnes couldn't help but wonder if the latter had exploited her opportunities here, perhaps as the niece of Mrs. Green she considered herself untouchable? As though the grace Henry extended to his housekeeper would cover her as well simply through association, no matter how she behaved.

Still, there was a sickness swelling in Agnes' core that she couldn't shake.

"Dear God," she whispered in her heart, "please don't take me away from Henry. I beg of You. Please... please God... forgive me... for everything."

The grandfather clock chimed twelve times and Miss Kingsley began to fuss. "If I don't get that bird cooked, there won't be a dinner at all."

The cook appeared flushed, but Agnes couldn't believe a sweet soul like Miss Kingsley could bring herself to steal anything. Besides, Agnes was sure that even if Miss Kingsley were to be found guilty, at this rate she'd likely finish preparing the dinner and bake an ample supply of raspberry tarts before she would permit herself to be arrested.

When the constable finally reached the first-floor landing once again, Henry's steps behind him were silent and heavy.

"Miss Agnes Archibald, you are under arrest," the constable proclaimed.

Horror struck her. She could not speak. How? This could not be. She was innocent. She knew she was innocent.

Lottie gasped for affect but Miss Kingsley was the only one in the trio who looked genuinely shocked. "Miss Agnes, no—"

When Henry finally emerged from the shadows, tears sheened his eyes. He held in his hands the papers she might once have had on her person back when she stole to survive—pawn duplicates. Only this time, she knew they did not belong to her.

The moment she met those immense ocean eyes of his, she pleaded with her own brewing with storms. "They're not mine," she whispered.

The constable twisted her arms back so hard she cried out.

"For goodness' sake, don't hurt her, man—" Henry's voice broke away.

The constable clamped cuffs on her wrists.

"They're not mine." She shook her head so viciously her cap flew off. "They're not mine."

The duplicates tumbled from Henry's fingers and fluttered to the floor, landing face up. To be sure, each one had her own name scrawled in condemning black ink.

"Come on, miss, there's no need to cause a scene," the constable said in undertones and pulled her toward the front door.

"Let me go!" Agnes writhed and stamped his foot with her own, trying to break free to run to Henry. "Please, believe me, those are not mine!"

A tear escaped down Henry's clean-shaven cheek, and he shook his head, stammering, "Your name is on every single one."

The constable grabbed hold of her and dragged her by the irons through the front door.

"Henry, they are not mine, I would never steal from you! Never." She sobbed as his pained face disappeared from her sight. "I love you—"

&

"God, what have I done?"

Henry sniffed back the tears threatening to suffocate him completely and stared at the empty doorway that screamed Agnes' absence.

"You can't blame yourself, sir," Mrs. Green said gently. "You weren't to know the woman was still a criminal."

"It's so terribly sad," Charlotte added, though her tone dripped with condescension.

Henry exhaled. "Cancel the dinner party."

Miss Kingsley stepped forward. "But sir—"

"I said cancel it, damnit!"

The three women stood wide-eyed. Silent.

Henry marched to his study, leaving the doors wide open, though no one dared follow. Wood grated against wood as he wrenched a drawer from the desk and threw it to the ground. Papers scattered. A lonely miniature portrait sat upon his carpet gazing back at him with the same grey eyes in which he'd just seen so much horror. He had not looked at the portrait of Josephine since the day Agnes had arrived. He remembered when his father had forced her to sit for it. She hadn't wanted to. There was a fire in that pale gaze that shone even through the small painting. It wasn't until his father had died and Henry inherited his estate that he found the portrait in his father's personal belongings.

Now, however, as he took in the portrait, he no longer saw Josephine. It was detailed enough to resemble her, but it was also obscure enough to be someone else entirely. He snatched it from the ground and cantered back to the hallway to retrieve the duplicates.

"Where are you going?" Mrs. Green asked softly, unmoved from her standing place.

But Henry could not respond in a gentlemanly enough manner, so he remained silent and stormed into the street prepared to enter the innerworkings of London's underground. He had done it before when he was a mere boy. He had fought for Josephine, certain she would be in danger or that her honor might be at stake, but this was different. This was Agnes and she hadn't just disappeared, she had been taken. If the allegations were true, then perhaps he could release this matter to God Almighty to deal with in His own divine plan. However, if the allegations were false, then Henry would fight with everything within him to set Agnes free. And this time, he had a paper trail he could follow.

The bell rang over the door of John Wentworth's pawnshop. The musty displays were filled with pawned—if not pilfered—goods. Brooches, gold watches, and silver boxes lined the most prominent display, while other less treasured trinkets were stacked in others.

Henry slid the miniature across the counter.

Without meeting his eye, Mr. Wentworth muttered. "Three shillings for the case. Take it or leave it."

"Have you seen this woman in the last week?" Henry demanded.

Mr. Wentworth adjusted his spectacles and sneered down at the portrait. "I haven't seen that girl in weeks. Though she wasn't cleaned up so nice last I did. Those eyes are hard to forget."

Henry Watson didn't have to be reminded of the fact. "But these duplicates here." He pulled them from his inside pocket. "They say they belong to an Agnes Archibald."

"People can give me any name, sir, I just write it down. Not my business."

"Look hard, man!"

Mr. Wentworth flinched and set his full attention on him.

"A woman's future depends on this," Henry said. "Do you remember the woman who sold you the silver spoons?"

"Course I do, I remember every customer who comes through, especially those who steal from the masters. That could be the only explanation for a set so fine. Here they are." He gestured to a blue velvet case. "Are you looking to buy them back?"

"I never want to see those cursed spoons again. But the woman, the woman who sold these to you, what did she look like?"

"Much older than the lass in the portrait."

Not Charlotte then. "Go on."

"She was well-to-do enough. Auburn hair, a grimace that could turn food sour, high thinking of herself."

Henry swallowed hard as he contemplated the unfathomable. "Did you happen to notice whether she wore a brooch?"

"Course I did, I offered to buy the thing. She wore it on her collar, a pearl the size of London in gold filagree."

It may have been an exaggeration but there could be no mistaking it. Henry had purchased that brooch for Mrs. Green the year she had turned sixty-years-old.

He cleared his throat. "Would you be willing to testify to the fact, sir?"

"I won't be getting on no court stand, Mr. Watson. I have a reputation to keep. I'd go out of business."

A shuddered breath dragged its way from Henry's chest. Agnes had been telling the truth. She was innocent. What was there to do about the matter if no witness came forward? Perhaps he could testify to her character? Perhaps he could force Mrs. Green to confess? But even then, now that the law had its greedy hands on Agnes, how would her prior crimes incriminate her still?

Chapter 9

Agnes' past came calling like an old lover set on revenge, dragging her to places she'd rather not remember and new ones she'd sooner not know. Grace, it seemed, was nowhere to be found in these God-forsaken places. All her hopes of being true and spotless were shattered—there was condemnation after all.

She had been delivered to Bow Street station house for processing before being stowed away in a damp dark holding cell at Newgate to await trial. Eight days she stayed in the small room with a bucket for her personal business, an armful of stale hay to sleep upon, and gruel served in a tin can. Agnes was determined not to cry. She wouldn't give the guards the satisfaction. They were leaving her alone for now, and that was the best she could expect for a woman in her vulnerable position.

A few days before Christmas, a police officer ushered her into the 'Old Bailey', London's Central Criminal Court. The frosty court room caused Agnes to shiver as she stood entirely alone at the prisoner's dock. With wide open windows, one might expect the room to at least hold some refreshment to it, but between the garlic and the carraway the judges and jury chewed in an attempt not to be contaminated by the diseased prisoners, the chilled air was rancid.

Her only comfort was the moment the courtroom filled with onlookers, and Henry Watson wove his way through the thralls of nosy Londoners to find a seat closest to the front. His iron gaze met hers from across the room and as she stood there trembling, he offered her the mildest of smiles. Agnes wanted to scream across the room and leap down from the dock and beg him to take her with him. But she knew all too well it was not to be.

"How will you be tried?" the clerk asked her.

She raised her dirt-stained hand. "By God and by my country," she replied softly, repeating the phrase an officer had taught her that morning.

Just as court was about to proceed, a barrister approached the bench. "Your Honor, I will be representing the defendant, Miss Agnes Archibald."

"Very well, Sir James," the judge grunted. His powdered wig hung clumsily over his shoulders and slipped slightly forward as he read over his notes.

Agnes' attention flew to Henry. She knew she could never afford legal counsel, not even with the wages she had saved. This could only have been Henry's doing.

When it was Sir James' turn to address the court, he presented the duplicates and retold a conversation between Mr. Watson and the pawnbroker. "Furthermore," said Sir James, "the broker confirmed the description of the woman who pilfered the items, and it did not fit Miss Agnes Archibald's description but rather than of Mr. Watson's own housekeeper, Mrs. Green, who had staged the incident entirely."

Shock seized Agnes. She might have suspected Lottie, but Mrs. Green?

"Has this Mrs. Green confessed to these allegations?" the judge asked nonchalantly.

"Only in a private conversation with Mr. Watson, your honor. However, she and her niece, who was also in his employment, have since disappeared."

"Disappeared?"

"Yes, Your Honor."

"How convenient." His double chin wobbled as he sighed. "Even if this extravagant explanation was the truth, we have several other accounts of theft attributed to this young woman. Do you have anything to respond to the three accounts of break-ins Agnes Archibald executed between the months of August and October of this year? Or the number of stolen items from local stores attributed to this young woman? Do you have anything to say on these matters?"

"Only that Mr. Henry Watson is willing to give an account of her exemplary character since commencing work in his house as a maid in November."

"Regardless of her references, Sir James, justice must be served, and this woman has a list of crimes for which she has not received due punishment."

Agnes stood silent. She clamped her stained hands together to keep them from trembling. She had never wanted Henry to see her like this, and here she was facing the possibility of never seeing him again. Perhaps her past would condemn her to Newgate Prison for the rest of her life. Everyone knew, after all, if a woman went to the 'Stone Jug', she never came out again unless it was to be hung or—

The jury huddled together in their box for a moment before nodding in agreement. The foreman then announced, "Guilty on all accounts."

Agnes' breath caught in her chest.

"Transported for seven years," the judge announced with a clip of his hammer. "Next case."

✷

Henry watched the fight leave Agnes Archibald's eyes as she was dragged away in cuffs. His insides twisted, his head growing light. An urge swelled within him, challenging him to fight for her but he knew it was of little use. This couldn't be happening. He was so sure that with his own barrister representing her, Agnes would be taken seriously. But the jury seemed to have pre-ordained her judgement, and the judge was not wasting any time to give it any further consideration.

When Henry returned to Mildred's Court, the house fell silent. Miss Kingsley met him in the hallway but one look from him confirmed his worst fears had transpired. Not only would Agnes be taken to Newgate Prison to wait out her sentence, but she would also then be transported to the other side of the world, and he would never see her again.

Without asking, Miss Kingsley substituted his cup of tea for a glass of port and placed it beside him at his desk.

"If I might be so bold, sir," Miss Kingsley began, "I have it on good authority Mrs. Fry does good work with the women at Newgate Prison."

His brow rose. "Yes, I do believe you are right."

"I know she's unlikely to play favorites, but I wonder if it's possible for you to put in a good word for Miss Agnes, so dear Mrs. Fry can see that she's looked after."

"Yes, of course. That's an exceptional idea, Miss Kingsley. Thank you. I shall call on her and Joseph this afternoon."

And he meant every word, though it was not Henry's primary objective for calling on his neighbors. He reached for a piece of parchment and his quill and began a letter he hoped would shed light into Agnes' hopeless situation. He cast all propriety aside as he began most affectionately with the words, *My dearest Agnes...*

Henry took time to pen his thoughts, his apology for not believing her, and his hopefulness for her future in the new land. He wondered if he might visit her before she was transported, if she could forgive him for questioning her loyalty, but would await her reply to do so.

He sealed the letter then walked a few houses down to visit Joseph and Elizabeth Fry and their eleven children who filled the house with laughter and beautiful chaos in a way he had never seen. Quickly, the children were taken by the Fry's housekeeper, and Henry sat down in the privacy of their drawing room to discuss the matter of Agnes Archibald.

"I am sorry to hear it," Elizabeth said, "Of course, I should be glad to keep my eye on her. I will be visiting Newgate myself again after Christmas."

Henry wished it could be sooner, he couldn't imagine Agnes spending Christmas alone in Newgate Prison, but he also knew there was little to be done. "I should like you to pass this on, if you would be so kind," he said softly, handing her the letter. "And if it's appropriate, I would like to say goodbye to her properly before she leaves."

"My dear man," Joseph began, a little aghast, a little impressed, "I do believe you are in love with this young woman."

Henry could not deny it. "Well, it won't do much to dwell on it now, but I should like to see her looked after as best I can. Even if it is from afar. If she has any needs... I'm not sure what can really be done..."

"I shall see to it," Elizabeth replied.

Henry stared into his untouched cup of tea. "I could have bribed the jury. Sir James said it often worked."

Elizabeth offered a knowing look.

"Could you though?" Joseph questioned.

"Never. Not in good conscience. Not in front of God Almighty who sees all."

"Well, there you have it. You did your best." Joseph took a sip of tea. "May our Lord have mercy on that poor woman."

Chapter 10

While most Londoners celebrated the wonder of Christmas, Agnes entered a living purgatory. Agnes no longer knew whether it was night or day, so dim were the corridors she now haunted. Beneath the ever-watchful eye of the jailer, she filed through bolted doorways and dark hallways into the heart of Newgate Prison where a matron waited to strip and search her. The matron then took notes of any distinguishing features.

"Grey eyes," the matron muttered beneath her breath. "No pockmarks."

When Agnes had been identified, she was given two pieces of sackcloth, a tin and a wooden spoon before the matron dismissed her for the next waiting prisoner.

Bile lurched into Agnes' mouth when the jailer shoved her into the women's common room and she was met with the putrid odor of nearly three hundred unwashed women and their excrements. Heavy metal groaned behind her and slammed shut with a force to put Lottie's poor attempts at closing a door to shame. Still, Agnes would do anything to put up with the young maid's taunting now. For instead, she was faced with countless eyes studying her. Some put the fear of God in her, and she wondered for what crime they had been arrested yet in the same moment didn't want to know. The cry of an infant pierced the shadows. And just when Agnes could not think of anything worse, she saw children huddled to their mothers, terrified. She remembered her own small self alone on the streets for the first time at fourteen. The same fear of the unknown blazed in their innocent eyes.

Agnes spotted the chamber pots lining the walls and wondered when they'd been emptied. Finding a patch of wall for herself, as far from the fresh stench as she could manage, she laid one piece of sackcloth on the floor, sat down, and covered herself with the other. Agnes clasped her tin and spoon with both hands. She could not bring herself to close her eyes that first night at Newgate Prison.

Each bleak morning that followed, the gruel was delivered in a great pot, and it was every woman for herself. Agnes learned quickly to dive and fight her way to her in to scoop gruel with her tin, and then scurry away to her place to make sure no one took her sackcloth. After breakfast, she would just sit silently and stare at the small, barred window that shed no more light than the eventide.

Agnes wasn't sure how many days had passed when a familiar face arrived at Newgate Prison. "The angel is here," one woman hissed to another. Agnes was surprised to discover Mrs. Elizabeth Fry from Henry's own social circle let through the heavy door and locked inside. Another equally elegant woman lingered in her shadow, helping Mrs. Fry carry the armfuls of clean green shifts she began to hand to the women.

Agnes watched Mrs. Fry step carefully between the women who didn't dare to rise, her purple boots and scarlet laces proving to be the brightest attraction in the room. When Mrs. Fry finally paused before Agnes, who like some others didn't want to assume the 'angel' held anything for her, she knelt down and placed the neat shift dress in Agnes' lap.

"My name is Mrs. Fry."

Agnes' fingers probed the green fabric, and she relished in its fresh scent. "I am Agnes Archibald."

"I was hoping I might find you," Mrs. Fry's voice reduced to a mere whisper. "I have something else for you. Pray tell, can you read?"

"Yes, ma'am."

"Very good." Mrs. Fry slipped a letter with Henry's own seal into the folds of green. "He would like to see you."

"Not like this." Agnes folded her bony hand around the fabric where the letter sat within. "Let him remember me as I was. He cannot see me like this."

"Read the letter, Miss Archibald. Perhaps it might change your mind."

"With all due respect, I am very grateful. But there is nothing he could say, short of announcing my freedom, that would make me change my mind, ma'am."

"Very well." Mrs. Fry gazed upon her, immense compassion in those small kind eyes. Then she asked the question, Agnes had heard her ask others in the room. "Tell me, is there anything you need?"

Agnes didn't have to think about it to know. "A penny, if you please."

A little startled by the request, Mrs. Fry's curiosity was evident. "Of course, but may I ask why?"

"I have none on my person, and I understand that through the underground workings here, there is someone who engraves pennies to leave as a token. I should like to have one made for Henry. I mean, Mr. Watson, ma'am."

"I am not in the habit of giving money directly in this place, but for this cause, I can make an exception." Mrs. Fry subtly took a penny from her coat pocket and stowed it away with the letter.

"Thank you, Mrs. Fry."

"And if you change your mind about seeing him, please do let me know."

"I am ever so grateful, ma'am, but believe me, I will not."

The next time Mrs. Fry came to visit, she brought with her fabric and needles and thread. She and her volunteers circulated the room, teaching the women how to wield the instruments and best use them to embroider and stitch fabric together. It was a skill Agnes had never mastered, being the daughter of a farmer, she had been worked on the land more than in the home. Though it was a pleasant distraction in a place void of all hope. Her fingertips stung with every false move, often staining the fabric she held, but it passed the time.

After devouring her main meal of bread and soup in the afternoon, Agnes Archibald joined the other women to hear scripture read aloud in the prison chapel. Believing she was well and truly forgotten by God this time, Agnes took to carving her name in one of the pews. At least then part of her would be remembered. Henry Watson would forget her soon enough, the streets of London would forget she was ever there, and she would be travelling across the world to a place she would no doubt once again feel invisible. Hope was a commodity she could not afford, and grace had forsaken her the moment she started to believe she was falling in love with Henry Watson.

She still couldn't bring herself to read his letter, nor the subsequent ones that followed. Though with the penny Mrs. Fry had given her she managed to have a token engraved with two hearts and the year that had been—1835. It was a year she would never forget. Its final two months, at least, were the most wonderful of her life.

She wasn't sure what his letters could have held, but she was terrified she would be dissatisfied with them. She wanted to remember Henry as the man who smiled at her from across the courtroom and brought a barrister to plead her case. She wanted to remember the sheen of his eyes when she was taken away, proof of his attachment to her. What if his letters were simply a goodbye, a wishing her well. It would fall on the broken shards of her heart and pierce her all over. No, she could not read them. Not yet.

Chapter 11

Spring had swept the frost from London and prepared the way for summer by the time Newgate Prison finalized their plans to release its prisoners to the sea. Though no one was told the day nor the hour.

It was a bleak July morning, in the darkest hours before dawn, and Agnes awoke to the sound of jarring metal. The iron bolts shuddered and a jailer snatched her from her patch of sackcloth on the floor. She was led through the desolate maze to the matron's quarters where her name was officially struck from Newgate's record. Agnes emerged from the prison's walls for the first time in months, her wrists and ankles aching beneath the weight of the irons, only to be bundled into a black carriage with boarded windows. Her eyes could scarcely focus as her body thumped between the wall of the carriage and the girl beside her.

Upon arriving at Woolwich docks, the carriage door flung open. Agnes kept her eyes screwed shut while she adjusted to the sudden brightness of daylight flooding the carriage. Once she dared to open them, she could scarcely bring herself to look down at her person. Even with the clean shift dress from Mrs. Fry, she was filthy beyond recognition. Her once thick hair was so matted and dull, she feared it would have to be shorn before too long lest the lice build nests and breed. Still, there had been a small remnant at one of the ends that held some luster, so she had asked Mrs. Fry if she might bring a pale blue ribbon on her last visit to Newgate Prison.

"Tell me, why blue?" Mrs. Fry had asked once she secured the small lock of chestnut hair.

"It was the color of my Sunday dress. That's how I want Henry to remember me. Please give it to him. And this..."

She had placed the token in Mrs. Fry's hand, convinced that she would never see the kind woman—nor Henry Watson—again.

Now, Agnes arrived at the docks with a sea of filthy women preparing to be herded onto the lowest decks of the ship. Navy officers whistled and cat-called from atop the enormous vessel at the sight of the fresh delivery of women. Agnes shivered as she filed down the dock and stepped into a small launch boat waiting to escort the women across the river Thames to where the *Westmoreland* sat anchored.

Once aboard, Agnes' irons were removed and the Surgeon Superintendent in full Navy regalia inspected her and took notes. He then offered her a sponge and a bucket of cold water to wash off the residue of Newgate Prison. When it came to her new boots, he held them up to better survey them and Agnes prayed he wouldn't find the letters from Henry stashed inside.

"Nice boots," he remarked and tossed them back to her.

After her first wash in months, Agnes breathed in the salty air and glanced at the ripples in the water before she and the other women entered the putrid bowels of the ship. She climbed into one of the berths, only 18-inches wide, and tried to get comfortable. Even with her small frame, her feet hung off the end. She curled up into herself and tugged the scratchy woolen blanket up to her chin. It wasn't for warmth so much as comfort, and in the miserable depths of the *Westmoreland*, Agnes shut her eyes tight and dared to hope against hope that where she was going would be at least better than here.

Five weeks passed on the ship and the *Westmoreland* didn't move till the captain finally announced one morning, after a final load of female convicts had boarded, that the vessel was indeed at capacity.

As the *Westmoreland* prepared to disembark, Agnes was busily scrubbing the top deck, a chore she was grateful for as she at least managed to see the sun, when another small boat approached. However, this one was not filled with more convicts to send the ship brimming over. No, it seemed Mrs. Fry and her volunteers were visiting the *Westmoreland* before its departure.

Soon the damp top deck was swarming with curious convict women. The Surgeon Superintendent called for order before commanding the women to file before Mrs. Fry and her volunteers. One by one each woman was gifted a Bible and a burlap bag filled with sewing supplies and patches of quilt. When Agnes received hers, Mrs. Fry whispered, "There is a final letter within."

That would make four. Four letters Henry had written her, but she dared not open. She dared not hope. What hope was there to have in this God-forsaken place?

She would never see Henry again, and nothing he could possibly say would change that fact.

"Please," Mrs. Fry added, "please read this one. It's important." She then laid her hand on Agnes' filthy hair and swiftly prayed over her. "Father God, go with this woman, I pray. May she discover the light of our Lord and Savior Jesus Christ in dark places, and may she experience the wonder of Your grace. Amen."

All other words caught in Agnes' throat till she managed to whisper a small, "Amen."

Then, Mrs. Fry took a numbered ticket upon a red ribbon and placed it over Agnes' head. The small tin ticket seemed deceptively heavy against her chest, and she peered down to survey it. She was number 227.

Once Mrs. Fry and her volunteers returned to their boat and disappeared into London's smog, Agnes finished scrubbing her portion of the top deck before returning to her berth. Her stomach growled in protest but rations were in short supply, and she would be lucky if she would be given an evening meal. Newgate's corruption seemed to have leaked onto the *Westmoreland*, and convict rations were often taken and given to the highest bidder.

Once in her berth, she began to look over the gifts. Another letter for her collection lay hidden within the

Bible, then a thimble, needles and thread within the bag along with fabric, and then there was the red ribbon that from this day forth would be tied around her neck. Where she was going, she would no longer be referred to as Agnes Archibald. No, she was no longer a young woman, according to those aboard the *Westmoreland*. She was #227.

"Can ye read that?" A mop of unruly red hair fell over the top bunk, and a pair of curious green eyes stared at her. "God's Word, I mean."

"Yes, I can read. My mam taught me before she passed on."

Tears pricked the young woman's eyes. "Would ye read to me? I'd appreciate it ever so much."

Agnes slowly nodded and cracked the good book open.

"Maybe a Psalm?" she asked in her thick brogue.

"I don't know what that is," Agnes confessed. The only part she was acquainted with of course was Romans.

"It's the poetry one."

Agnes began to flick through the pages till she eventually found the requested book. She cleared her throat and began to read aloud, albeit softly.

"O LORD God of my salvation, I have cried day and night before thee..."

The redhead looked far off in contemplation. Her cheek pressed to the edge of her berth above. "Go on," she whispered.

"Let my prayer come before thee: Incline thine ear unto my cry; For my soul is full of troubles: And my life draweth night unto the grave."

Tears rolled down her cheeks as she listened. "Please, do go on."

"Are you sure? I don't want to upset you."

She shook her head once and continued to lay half-hanging from the top berth.

"Very well." Agnes sighed. She couldn't think of anything more depressing than reading such poetry but figured it would at least fill some time. *"I am counted with them that go down into the pit: I am as a man that hath no strength."* Her chin wobbled slightly over the words but she steeled her jaw and continued. *"Free among the dead, like the slain that lie in the grave, whom Thou rememberest no more: And they are cut off from Thy hand."* Agnes had never read such words of complaint toward God, but then thought if the complaints of this poet were in the Bible, then perhaps He might hear her cries too. *"Thou has laid*

91

me in the lowest pit, In darkness, in the deeps. Thy wrath lieth hard upon me, and Thou hast afflicted me with all Thy waves." Her voice grew louder. "Thou has put away mine acquaintance far from me; Thou hast made me an abomination unto them: I am shut up, And I cannot come forth." She quickened and her heart began to pound within her chest. "Mine eye mourneth by reason of affliction: LORD, I have called daily upon thee, I have stretched out my hands unto thee. Wilt Thou shew wonders to the dead? Shall the dead arise and praise thee? Shall they lovingkindness be declared in the grave? Or they faithfulness in destruction? Shall they wonders be known in the dark? And Thy righteousness in the land of forgetfulness?"

She glanced up to see several pairs of gaunt eyes staring at her, hanging on her every word as she read the prayer of their hearts.

"But unto thee had I cried, O LORD," she went on softly, "And in the morning shall my prayer prevent thee..."

A shuddered breath escaped her chest.

"Beautiful," the redhead said, and the other women turned their attention away. "I'm 293, by the way."

"I'm 227, but my name is Agnes."

A small smile ignited the young woman's face. "I'm Bridget."

In the foggy hours that summer morning, Henry rode toward Woolwich docks and prayed he was not too late. Business in Bath and settling of his accounts had consumed months of his time, and there was still so much yet to be done. But if he could just see her one more time before she departed, he would try to be content. If only she would read his blasted letters. The woman was so stubborn, resigned to the hopelessness of the situation. He shook his head and fought back a smile. Yes, stubborn, and strong, and fierce, yet gentle when she wanted to be.

The stallion's hooves thundered up the wharf only for them to be slowed by the descending crowds. Henry searched the misty water that glimmered in the first light of the day to see the *Westmoreland* easing into its stride along the river. His heart sank within him, and the horse slowed to a halt. He was too late.

"Good morning, Mr. Watson." Elizabeth Fry walked the short way from the wharf toward her carriage. "I have something for you."

Henry dismounted his horse and took hold of the reins before striding over to meet her. "Good morning,

Mrs. Fry. I don't suppose you have news of Miss Archibald?"

"More than that." She reached into her purse to reveal a penny and a lock of hair tied in blue ribbon. "This is something the women do," she said gently, "to be remembered."

She placed the small items in Henry's waiting palm.

Gazing intently at the gifts, he traced a fingertip over the engraved penny—two hearts and the year 1835. Folding his hand around it, he tucked the items securely away in his interior pocket. "Thank you, Mrs. Fry."

"She had quite insisted upon it, down to the shade of the ribbon."

His hand instinctively rested upon his chest where the lock of hair lay hidden. "Yes, it was the color of her Sunday dress."

She smiled. "You remember."

"How could I forget?"

Part Two

Chapter 12

DECEMBER 1836, VAN DIEMEN'S LAND

The *Westmoreland* chased summer from one side and of the world to the other for five long months until the North Star could no longer be seen, and a constellation known as the Southern Cross spread across the sky.

With unsteady legs, Agnes joined the file of convict women. She held Bridget's hand tight within her own and took in this new world. In the distance, she spotted large, strange animals with enormous tails. They hopped near the riverside, upon their hind legs, before disappearing into the foliage of the forest. Black swans with red beaks sailed the river and foreign birds and a few seagulls littered the sky. Men tripped over one another on the docks, all trying to best see the fresh importation of women in Van Diemen's Land. Agnes shuddered. At least on the *Westmoreland*, she had been able to go beneath the notice of male attention once she had made it clear she was uninterested in using 'favors' to buy more rations or other luxuries. She had been mostly left alone thereafter, for there were plenty of women all too willing to oblige— the countless pregnant women surrounding her testified to the fact. But this was different. A fire burned in the eyes of these men, and they looked hungry for more than food and that terrified her.

She kept her head down, trying to ignore the cat calls and obscene hand gestures, and focused on breathing in the fresh rain-scented air and the feeling of earth beneath her feet. For summer, it was surprisingly cold on this southern island. Grey clouds brewed overhead, and she expected them to open at any moment. Despite the chill crawling up her skin, endless beauty surrounded her. The landscape of Van Diemen's Land was so lush, it even smelled green. Beyond the port and the township, a great mountain covered in forest rose before them and the scarlet-clad guards marched the women up Macquarie Street toward it.

Bridget trembled beside her. The poor girl was only here because she stole a loaf of bread to feed her younger siblings. It had been her first offence, but her trial, Bridget explained, had been at the end of the day when the judge was exhausted from sentencing and in a foul disposition, and some of the jury members were even drunk or nose-deep in a newspaper. Bridget received the harshest sentence imaginable for her one-off crime. She was to be transported for seven years. It was a life sentence, just like Agnes, for neither would ever be able to afford to return to their homeland.

In the town built on the backs of convicts, the women were marched past St David's Church and Agnes dared a glance up at the stucco-covered cathedral. She remembered Mrs. Fry's final prayer over her, for Jesus to shine His light in dark places. The weathered Bible still weighed down Agnes' small sack of belongings. She had been careful to bring it to the top deck on occasion for the sun to dry its pages, lest they be lost to mildew like so many of the other women's. She wasn't even sure why she had bothered, but from that first day of the voyage when she had read Psalm 88 aloud to Bridget, something had changed. Agnes decided from that moment that she would go to God with her complaints, much like the poet had done. What could it hurt? If she tested His patience, He could always strike her down with lightning and end her misery. Though, so far, He had not. She even sensed at times as though He was listening.

Agnes wasn't sure what the significance was of St David, but as they passed the building, Bridget released Agnes' hand to make the sign of the cross upon herself. Agnes figured it couldn't hurt and tried to copy the gesture. She was certain she had it all wrong, or at least the mirth in Bridget's eyes told her she did, but in her heart she told God she was trying, and she liked to think He understood.

With the industry and noise of the shipping port now behind them, the women struggled up the muddy mountain side where the river thinned and all Agnes could see amongst the foreign flora and fauna was the occasional wood house or stone water mill. Her sea-legs ached beneath her and her now threadbare shift did little against the winds barreling through the great valley. Then the skies opened and poured down on them.

"*Yea, though I walk through the valley of the shadow of death, I will fear no evil,*" Bridget whispered against the grey, her slick hand grasping Agnes' all the tighter. "*for Thou art with me; they rod and they staff they comfort me...*"

Agnes offered a mild reassuring smile to Bridget, threading her arm through hers to steady her as they entered a hollow. There, hidden in the cliffs of Mt Wellington, stood Cascades Female Factory, surrounded by twenty-foot stone walls.

The matron met them at the entrance before she permitted her scraggly husband, the superintendent, to read from the 'Rules and Regulations for the Management of the House of Correction for Females'.

"There is to be no talking," he said solemnly, "no laughing, no singing..."

The list went on until Agnes' feet felt like they made explode from her old faithful boots. If Newgate Prison had been purgatory, then Agnes was sure this place was a living hell.

∽

Henry Watson was never one to believe in superstition. When the sailors of the *William Metcalfe* feared Friday was an ominous day to embark on their quest, the captain declared it all to be nonsense. However, two months into their journey, working class and upper class alike were struck will illness, the infirmary was overflowing with diseased patients, and ten children had already been buried at sea.

"What on earth is a man like you doing on a ship like this." The doctor shook his head as he inspected the inside of Henry's mouth. "There are families ready for a new life, women looking for husbands, but a gentleman like you, Mr. Watson, I don't entirely understand."

Henry swallowed past the pain and the taste of blood, while the doctor rummaged in his kit. "Would you laugh if I told you it was for a woman?"

"Only while you're not looking."

"Well, there you have it. I have sold everything I own and am sailing to a foreign land in search of a woman."

"Does the lucky woman know?"

He winced as the doctor prodded at his bleeding gums. "No," he answered finally when he could swallow once more. "Or at least, I don't think so. I wrote her, but I don't think she read my letters."

"If she won't read your letters, how do you know she wants to see you again?"

"She left me a token," he said softly. "I understand she just doesn't want to hope."

"Hope can be dangerous if put in the wrong subject, certainly. For instance, if you hoped I could help you but I was not a qualified physician, then that would indeed be hopeless."

"But I am hoping you *are* a qualified physician."

"Well, in this instance your hope is not in vain, and I will administer lime juice for treatment. As for the woman, I fear I don't have any helpful advice. They have never been my area of expertise."

Chapter 13

"And pray tell, 227, what are these?" the matron sneered as she pilfered Agnes' bag.

Agnes gasped when the matron discovered her collection of envelopes and she leapt to their defense. "No, don't—"

With a single glance from the matron, the superintendent took hold of Agnes' arms. Now that Agnes was dressed in the prison uniform, complete with apron, cap, and fresh stockings, it was apparently the matron's prerogative to determine whether the rest of her belongings would be required for the duration of her sentence. The matron had simply nodded upon discovering the Bible and returned it to its place, but she seemed to take an interest in these.

"Letters?"

"Please. They're all I have left."

"But they haven't even been opened. Can't you read, girl?"

"Of course, I can."

"Well, so can I." The matron tore the top one and read aloud, brief and tight, almost sucking the affection out of Henry's penmanship. Almost. *"Dearest Agnes, this will now be my fourth and final letter to you. I had hoped you might have replied, that I might have visited you before you departed, but I see now that was not meant to be. You see, I needed to feel your absence so acutely that I would be forced to take action. So, my dear Agnes, I am coming,"* she paused and glanced up at Agnes then back to the letter. *"On the 7th of October the William Metcalfe will be setting sail for Van Diemen's Land, and I shall be on it. I pray you will forgive me for all that transpired and that one day we shall be reunited. Yours, Henry."* She stared at the letter long and hard. "Who is this Henry Watson?"

Hope filled Agnes till she couldn't contain it and it spread across her dirt-stained face, like a light in a dark place. "What does it matter? He is coming for me."

The matron took the letters and tore them into pieces.

"No!"

"Seven years," the matron reminded her, "seven years you owe to the Crown, so whether he is coming or not, Henry Watson will have to wait till then."

"He'll buy me if he has to," Agnes retorted, struggling against the superintendent's claws. "He's sailing across the world to be with me, he will find a way."

"Silence," she thundered. "We already have a master in mind for you. One who will break you in, you evil wretch!"

Agnes shut her mouth for fear of stoking the matron's fire.

Silence it seemed would pervade every aspect of Agnes' foreseeable future. From the supper of ox head soup and hard brown bread to the mandatory chapel service led by Cascades' own reverend, and then to the sleeping quarters where hammocks hung so close there was no way of walking between them—nor getting in them without a great deal of effort. All of this was done in silence. Though she soon recognized the knowing looks of the more experienced women, particularly those who wore a yellow 'C' on their cap, petticoat, and sleeve. The Cascades' uniform was bland in every way, so the bright color drew attention. It didn't take long for Agnes to realize these were the rebels of Cascades, one of them scrawled in the hymnal two words 'Flash Mob'. She wasn't sure if it was an offer to join them in their plans, but while Agnes and the other newcomers tried to sleep that night, the Flash Mob pulled tobacco and alcohol from their sacks and took it to the front gate. Agnes followed, curious, till the guard took the bait and let the women escape for the night. Agnes slunk back to her hammock for fear of being caught but the Flash Mob women returned come morning, breathless, trying not to laugh, and reeking of alcohol and men.

Breakfast meant more watery ox head soup followed by another mandatory chapel service. Then, the women with the yellow 'C' were sent to the stone washtubs to scrub the convict men's clothes clean, while Agnes lined up in the interior yard amongst a group of women. She hadn't spoken to Bridget since their walk up the base of the mountain, but now they stood a few feet apart, a silent fear coursing between them.

Before her personal audience with the matron, Agnes had assumed she would serve her seven years at Cascades. But now she feared which brute of a master would be taking her home. Wagons arrived by nine in the morning, while other groups came on foot, all surveying the latest produce as though they were at the market and the women were for sale.

"Mr. Tucker," the matron began, "this is the girl I mentioned. Number 227."

Agnes peered up into the flushed red face of Mr. Tucker. He reeked of whiskey and his eyes could scarcely focus on her face. She shuddered inside as terror rose like bile in her throat.

"Don't ye have a real name, lass?"

"Not anymore."

He rolled his eyes. "Well, 227 it is."

Before she could whisper her goodbye to Bridget, his calloused hand wrapped around her wrist and every saving grace was dashed when he avoided the wagons and opted for the sloppy makeshift road.

"Keep up will ye." He yanked her arm so hard she thought it may pop from its place.

Her heart pounded in her ears. Soon it was all she could hear.

The man wore a constant grimace and Agnes didn't want to imagine the hours that were to come in this man's presence.

He dragged her through the sludge toward the outskirts of town, where a lone cottage sat without a patch of garden. Mr. Tucker ploughed through the front door and, once inside, finally released his hold.

"Kitchen's through there. Wood's out back. Behave yerself."

She swallowed hard.

"And I'm hungry." He grunted and strode to the adjoining sitting room.

Agnes stood there stunned for a moment. She had heard wretched tales of drunken men over the years and figured it was only a matter of time before Mr. Tucker tried to exert his power over her. Still, while he was content to simply be fed, she'd feed the blasted fellow night and day if she had to.

Agnes found the kitchen and made swift work of a simple supper of a few vegetables, bread, and cheese. She found a bottle of whiskey and poured him a glass. If she had to bide her time with Mr. Tucker till Henry arrived, then so be it. She would behave herself so long as the man kept his hands to himself. If he crossed that line, she wouldn't hold herself responsible for her actions.

The vegetables she found were on the turn, so she stoked the stove till it burned good and hot, and cooked them down into a sort of stew. It was a trick she had learned from Miss Kingsley, when they were no good for roasts, she'd stew them and no one would be none the wiser that it wasn't the freshest of produce.

Agnes delivered Mr. Tucker's plate to him then stood back, awaiting further instruction.

"I'll be off to the pub tonight." He swigged his whiskey before starting his meal. "There's a room off the kitchen for ye. Make sure ye bolt the door behind me, lass. And don't let no one in."

"What about you?" she asked quietly.

"I won't be back till mornin' anyway. Got meself a missus of sorts in town."

"Oh."

He took a wide bite of cheese and bread. "So ye see, 227. I mean ye no harm. Just need a bit of help is all."

Agnes' insides thawed and she stepped into the candlelight. "Mr. Tucker?"

He grunted and shoveled the vegetables into his mouth.

"My name is Agnes."

He swallowed his full mouth with a wince. "Well, Miss Agnes. Ye make a mighty good stew, I'll give ye that."

The corner of her mouth tilted. "Thank you, sir."

"Nah, none of that sir nonsense. Just call me Tuck. And remember what I said about that door, won't ye? Ye don't let no one in. Even if they say they're me. The men'll know I've got a lass back at the house now and I don't want no trouble with ye getting knocked up and the like."

She flinched. "Believe me, Tuck. I have no intention of getting involved with any of the men here."

And it was true, because as far as she could calculate from the seventh of October, Henry would not arrive for some time.

"May I ask why you're here?" Agnes asked.

"I've done me time, Miss Agnes. I got caught thieving to feed my family."

"You... you had a family back home?"

He tapped his whiskey glass, and she quickly went to refill it. "Wife. Three boys. One daughter. They'd be grown now. She'd probably be "bout yer age."

Agnes fought the tears aching for release. "I'm so sorry, Tuck."

"Yeh, well, I'm sure ye've got yer own sad tale."

"I dare say I have."

"Well, no good dwellin' on it eh?" He stood and emptied his glass. "Ye get a few drags of that whiskey in ye, and ye'll forget all about him."

"How do you know it's about a man?"

Tuck returned his hat to his mop of grey hair and staggered toward the door. "Yer a young lass. It's always about a man."

Agnes bit back a smile.

"Now, lock the door ye hear?"

He sounded aggressive in his order, but Agnes assumed it was the gentlest he knew how to be. "I'll be sure to do that, Tuck."

"Well, "night then." He tapped his hat and disappeared into the dark.

As instructed, Agnes bolted the front door then double checked all the windows before taking the lamp to her quarters. It was nothing like her room at Mildred's Court, but it was significantly better than anywhere she had slept in the last year. After scrubbing her filthy self with the water left over from the stove and an old boot brush she found in the kitchen, she retrieved her second Cascades' shift from her sack. It was as irritating as poison ivy but at least it was clean. She fell into the bed and brought the woolen blanket up to her chin.

Agnes leapt out of bed at the first lot of banging on the door. She waited for it to stop before returning to her bed. She jolted at the second lot and rolled her eyes.

These men were desperate for female company but so long as she had the protection of Tuck and his solid front door, she shouldn't need to worry.

By the third time, she screamed from her bed. "Push off!"

And with a mumble and a few curse words, the drunk young man did.

Chapter 14

When Tuck didn't return the following morning, Agnes distracted herself with chores, taking initiative to clean what was dirty and mend what was torn with the sewing supplies in her sack. She took her concern out on the pile of wood out the back of the cottage, and over the course of the morning mastered the swinging of the axe till she split the logs in perfect pairs. It was nearing midday when the crunch of dried twigs forced her to spin around, axe at the ready.

She gasped. "Bridget?" Dropping the tool to the ground, she hastened toward her red-headed friend whose skin was black and blue. Bridget's left eye swelled and distinct purple handprints marked her arms. "Who did this to you?"

Bridget shook her head. "I shouldn't even be here, but I had to warn ye. They're comin' for ye Agnes, ye have to get out of here."

"What do you mean? Who's coming?"

"Yer Mr. Tucker fell drunk off the wharf last night, they found him this mornin'. "Tis not safe here anymore for ye, Agnes. I heard me master talkin' with the boys, and they're plannin' on takin' ye tonight."

"I've locked the door." She shook her head and stepped away. "They can't get in..."

"All that was savin' ye was that they'd have to answer to Mr. Tucker for a broken window." Bridget's eyes pleaded with her. "I have to go now. Please, Agnes, get out while ye can. Go back to Cascades. Just go."

Before Agnes could conjure a response, Bridget disappeared. Swiping the axe into her grip, Agnes marched inside and locked the door behind her. Her heart thudded in her chest. Tuck was dead. Henry was still on the sea. And Bridget, her only friend, was in a far worse situation than Agnes had been till now. Now, Agnes didn't know what to think or what to do. Could she even make her way back to Cascades on her own? She just needed to bide her time till Henry arrived, but God only knew how long that would take.

"God," she whispered.

Rummaging through her sack, she emptied its contents onto the bed and picked up her Bible. She didn't know what to read so she simply clung to it and pressed it into her chest.

"God, please. Help me. Tell me what to do. Rescue me now and I will follow You anywhere."

Agnes kissed the book then returned it to her sack along with necessary items, before raiding the kitchen for any food. She rummaged through Tuck's bedroom and pulled out clean clothes. Certainly, a woman running through the woods would draw attention, but a young woodcutter, surely not. He was a great deal larger than she but with a few stitches, a belt, coat, and hat, Agnes hid whatever femininity she possessed and looked the part. Slinging her sack over her shoulder and retrieving the axe, she used the back door and trudged through the bare yard that led to the edge of the forest. Once under the cover of the foliage, she ran for her life.

Tall grey trees marked her journey into the foreign wilderness and those same large, strange animals hopped out of sight quicker than she could work out what they were. Enormous rabbits, perhaps? If that was the case, maybe she could chase one down and cook it for supper.

But as the sun descended on Van Diemen's Land and Agnes became lost in foreign territory, she would have to make do with bread and cheese, for no bounding animals returned.

Not wanting to draw unnecessary attention to herself, she forewent a fire and found a hollow tree to curl up in. It looked blackened from flames, and she remembered the stories they told on the *Westmoreland* of the natives burning off forest land and other strange occurrences. Agnes began to wonder of the natives, she hadn't seen one since arriving, but she could not blame them the way the men spoke of hunting them for sport. Agnes felt as though she had more in common with the native folk here than her own fellow British man, who seemed to view her in much the same way. She was a sport. Prey to be hunted. But little did they know, she would fight them till the death.

❧

Somewhere over the Indian Ocean, Henry leaned against a barrel on the top deck, his Bible splayed open before him. He peered up, squinting across the horizon, watching the clouds turn from indigo to blazing amber.

First light ignited the words on the page, and he leaned in to read from the book of second Corinthians. *"Therefore if any man be in Christ, he is a new creature: old things are passed away; behold all things are become new."*

"All things," he whispered.

With all the bed rest he had been prescribed, he had had a lot of time to consider the events of last December, from Agnes' confession of loyalty to Mrs. Green's heinous crime against her. He desperately wanted 'all things' to include Agnes Archibald. Situation had made her a thief, but it was never who she was, and now her condemnation came when she had been blameless.

What was the point of it all? He didn't understand. How could God allow both their young lives to be so traumatized and then bring them together just to tear them apart once more?

"Please, Lord, help me understand," he said softly, "because right now I am trying not to be angry. I am trying to hold onto hope. I am trying—"

Stop trying.

The two words resonated in his spirit.

Stop. Trying.

Henry sighed and remembered aloud, *"For by grace are ye saved through faith; and that not of yourselves... it is the gift of God... Not of works, lest any man should boast..."*

He had held onto that verse for years when he could not overcome the nightmares. No matter how hard he tried. He took all the long walks, drank all the port the doctor recommended, and it turned out to be counterproductive. Then he began to pray about it. He gave it to God and confessed he could not battle them on his own anymore. And the Lord took over.

When the nightmares started again that November, he tried to distance himself from Agnes, only to sense this divine pull toward her. Whenever he stopped trying and allowed himself to feel it, he saw glimpses into her beautiful soul. Soon the nightmares transformed into dreams, and it was no longer Josephine he was searching for on the streets, almost terrified of what he might find. No, it was Agnes. He never imagined those dreams would become a reality. At least, he hoped reality reflected what he could have never allowed himself to confess to Agnes. He would search for her in those dreams, and he would find her, beyond all harm and degradation, and he would take her in his arms. Then, he would wake up. The dreams faded after a while but since being on the ship they had started again, more vivid than ever before.

Chapter 15

When Agnes awoke the following morning, she was not alone. First light pierced through the trees, igniting the mist and the silhouette of a great creature. Its strong neck bent down low to nibble the wild grass glistening with dew. Agnes' eyes fluttered open, but she dared not move, till footsteps alerted the beast and sent it bounding off into the forest. A gun shot pierced the air, followed by a grunt.

"Blasted "roo, missed it," the man muttered.

Agnes curled deeper into the hollow and kept her hat down, praying not to be noticed.

He cocked his gun. His footsteps felt a breath away. She squeezed her eyes tight, listening. Somehow in the last year, Agnes' hearing had improved. In all the dark places she had found herself, where she could no longer rely on her eyes, she would listen. In Newgate Prison in the middle of the night, she would listen to the madwomen and hope she wasn't their next target. In the four-foot berths of the *Westmoreland*, in the shadows of the vessel's bowels, with no light and the door bolted shut, she would listen to make sure no one unlocked that door. She began to learn the officers shifts, when one would leave his post and another would resume, and she listened for it before she gave way to sleep. At Cascades Female Factory she had listened with intrigue to the comings and goings of the Flash Mob, carefully out of step with the matron's impromptu inspections. In that small room beyond Tuck's kitchen, she had listened to the men driven mad with lust inevitably stalking away down the street, back to the pub from which they came.

She found she could still her racing mind, her thrashing heart, and all would be supernaturally clear.

Agnes listened as the man's footsteps veered east, and she exhaled. Before chancing another encounter, she pulled herself together and headed west toward the river. Dawn rose over the distant harbor and Agnes stilled for a moment, overcome by wonder. She hadn't noticed yesterday in the dimming light how far she had climbed but from half-way up the mountain, the view was breathtaking. Misty ocean stretched to the horizon, the town seemed insignificant in its lush surroundings. Trees with grey-blue leaves reached toward the low cloud cover across the mountain top and in the distance the sound of water rushing travelled on the wind. Agnes had heard of the arid heat of Australia, but here in Van Diemen's Land, even the summer felt cool—like home.

By midday, however, the Southern sun proved Agnes was not home, nor would she ever be, and she reached the river in time to cool her face and have a deep drink of the fresh mountain water. Never had she tasted water so sweet, and so busy was she in her own world of wonder, that she didn't hear the commotion inside the nearby wooden cottage till it was too late.

"Hey boy! Chop those logs, would ye?" the woman called across the open space. "I'll give ye two shillings."

Agnes tapped the tip of her hat as she'd seen Tuck do, then reached for her axe. The wood was piled closer to the house than she would have liked, but two shillings were two shillings.

She squinted against the sun and got to work. Her arms ached from the efforts of yesterday but if she was going to survive—and by George, she would survive—then she had to push herself beyond her limits.

"God," she whispered, "please help me."

She swung the axe straight and hard, splitting the logs in perfect pairs. How she wished she could remove her coat, but she couldn't risk anyone seeing more of her petite frame than necessary. As it was she looked like a boy of fourteen. So she could only imagine the welcoming she would receive if someone discovered she was instead a woman of eighteen. Her eighteenth birthday had come and gone on the *Westmoreland*, not that there was anything to show for it. But she knew, and that was all that mattered.

The afternoon dragged on and once she completed the work, she marched up the steps with a confidence she didn't own, and kept her head down.

"Fine work, boy," the woman remarked. "Two shillings, as promised."

Agnes held out her hand only to have the woman grab hold of her. With her free hand, the woman tapped beneath the rim of Agnes' wide hat. Agnes' fierce grey eyes glared but came across a round cheery face.

"I thought as much." The woman placed the two shillings in Agnes' hand then nodded. "Best ye come in then."

Agnes followed the woman into the simple wooden cottage filled with the scent of freshly baked bread.

"Fancy a cuppa tea?"

Agnes took a tentative step. "If you know I'm lying, why are you helping me?"

Her hands paused on the lid of the teapot. "Because I was like ye once, and I wish someone had the guts to help me back then. Now, take ye coat off. We won't be disturbed here. Everyone thinks Mr. Richards is a woodchopper."

"If he's not a woodchopper, what is he?"

"Dead. God rest his soul. But no one knows it."

"I've had my fill of dead men for one day, let me tell you." Agnes sighed.

"Did yer man die too?"

"No, but my master did. If ye can call him that."

She began to boil the water. "Ye from Cascades then?"

Agnes nodded.

"Better there than the way I had it." She nodded to the dining table. "Take a seat, love, and I'll make us some food."

"I can't thank you enough," Agnes said, but her mind was still stuck back in Cascades. "You weren't sent to Cascades then?"

"It wasn't around in my day. I was sent here, the minute I got off the ship I was bought with a bottle of whiskey and Mr. Richards dragged me up here."

"I'm sorry."

"To the world I'm Mrs. Richards, always have been. At least his name protected me from other men, if not from him. But I used to go by Cherry. I looked like one see, always been red-faced and round, and I used to make a decent cherry pie."

The kettle almost boiled over, and Cherry quickly retrieved it with a thick towel before pouring it into the pot.

"I'm Agnes, by the way."

"Well, make sure you don't tell anyone else ye real name. Ye don't know who to trust in these parts. Do ye have a nickname? A surname?"

"Archibald."

"There now." She nodded once. "I'll call ye Archie."

"I've been called worse."

Cherry laughed heartily as she brought the tray to the table.

"So, may I ask how Mr. Richards died?"

She shrugged. "Roo hunting."

"What's a roo?"

"*Kanga-roo*—it's a whopping big jumping thing with a huge tail, bounds about on its hind legs and carries its babies in its pouch. Quite incredible."

"Kangaroo," Agnes whispered.

"Mr. Richards was after one himself, but he got shot by another hunter. I think the man was too ashamed to report it, and it was too convenient for me not to report it, so I buried him and that was that."

"Still, it takes a strong woman to bury a dead man."

"Not when yer life depends on it, Archie. When it comes to survival, sometimes a woman needs to do just about anything. Like pretend to be a man and chop wood for money."

A hint of a smile tilted Agnes' mouth as she took her first sip of tea since Mildred's Court. Her senses awakened, and the warmth penetrated her to her core.

"If ye keep chopping wood for me, Archie, I'll make sure ye have ye tea and bread every day."

She nodded. "I'd be happy to, Mrs. Richards."

Chapter 16

JANUARY 1837, VAN DIEMEN'S LAND

New Year's celebrations looked different this year while Henry recovered from his bout of scurvy. He was constantly in and out of the infirmary, first for treatment, then with infected gums. He sucked as many limes as rations would allow, before moving onto the lemons. Wincing against the sour juice, he was on the top deck when the long-awaited announcement finally arrived—

Land ahead.

His first glimpse at this strange new world was one of utter wonder. He had never seen so much green, nor had he tasted such clean sweet air. To think Agnes was hidden within that landscape. He couldn't imagine what her journey must have been like, a passenger ship was known to be more comfortable than a convict one, and as it was the passengers had endured horrific storms, seasickness, and disease. How his body longed for steady ground.

The women and children were the first to leave the ship, crowded into launches that were tied to the wharf on the other end while emptied. The sailors then returned for the next lot. As a single gentleman, Henry was one of the last to arrive on the docks of Hobart Town.

A young man wielding a sign with the name 'Watson' scrawled upon it leaned on one of the posts but leapt to attention at the sight of him. "Mr. Watson, sir?"

"Yes, indeed."

The man smoothed his brown waistcoat before retrieving Henry's case.

"What might your name be?"

"Tobias Woodhouse, sir. But just call us Toby."

"Very good, Toby. It's nice to meet you."

"This way, sir," Toby nodded in the direction of the street. "The place is all ready for you."

Henry Watson took in the sights of government house with its zoo of unusual native animals—one extremely large bird with bulging eyes was perhaps the most fierce of the lot—and took a turn past the cathedral until they arrived at a neat townhouse that still smelled of fresh paint.

"I can make a simple breakfast," Toby began, "but if you want yourself a proper woman like, you may want to call on Cascades Female Factory. They're convicts, of course, but any I've met have been bricky girls, really."

"Have you met many?"

"Only those that sneak out to go to the pub at night. No one knows how they do it, but folk around here call them the Flash Mob, a bunch of rebels."

Henry's lips twitched. "Perhaps, once I've settled, you can take me to—"

"Cascades. It used to be a distillery, see, till it became a prison."

"I see."

The master bedroom of the house was small compared to what Henry was accustomed to, but it was new and clean and scented with fresh wood from the furnishings. He unpacked his own things into the drawers of the dresser, something he wasn't practiced in but found simple enough, and then went to find Toby in the kitchen.

"Tea, sir?"

"Please."

Henry sat at the table and watched the young man at work. He couldn't have been more than twenty. "So, what's your story, Toby?"

"No story, sir."

"Everyone has a story."

He shrugged. "Mama was sent here, and I was young enough to be sent too."

"Does your mother live in town?"

"No, she died, sir. On the voyage over."

"I am so sorry. You must have been incredibly young then."

"Yes, sir. Not eight years old." He shrugged. "A family took me in when I arrived, made sure I was raised good and proper and the like. So, it's not all bad."

Henry nodded thoughtfully and sipped his tea. He wasn't sure if it was the travel or if this was genuinely the most delicious tea he had ever tasted, but whatever it was, it was a slice of heaven. "Toby, this tea is extraordinary."

"I was also taught to make a decent cuppa." He grinned. "Drink up, sir, then I'll take you up to Cascades."

The sun was high by the time they arrived at the bleak fort in the cliffs of Mt Wellington. A fire ignited within Henry as he descended the carriage and marched up to the looming entrance. Stone walls overshadowed everything within, casting an ominous heaviness. He was met with silence. He glanced at the women scrubbing clothes in the hard stone washtubs, desperate to see a tendril of chestnut curls peeking out from one of the bonnets, or for his gaze to be met by those grey eyes he had missed so dreadfully.

The matron in stiff woolen clothes and a white bonnet stormed from inside one of the buildings. "Can I help you?"

"Good morning, madam. This gentleman just arrived and requires some help in the home, if you have someone suitable," Toby said.

"Actually, I am looking for one in particular," Henry spoke up. "I believe her number is 227." He cringed at the use of it but was also grateful Mrs. Fry had offered him the foreknowledge.

"227 is no longer with us."

Henry's brow creased. "Then where is she?"

"She is missing, sir."

"I don't understand. She was transported here."

She released a mighty sigh. "227 was employed with a Mr. Tucker but the man drowned in his own drunken state, and before we could retrieve her from the house, she was gone."

"I heard about Mr. Tucker. Bit rough around the edges, but a decent fellow," Toby offered. "Certainly, didn't deserve to go the way he did."

Henry stared at the matron. "And has nothing been done to recover her?"

"This is a dangerous land, sir. If she has run away, she's likely to be dead."

"Then you do not know Agnes Archibald."

A look of recognition flashed across her countenance. "I see, and you must be Mr. Watson."

Heat crawled up his neck. "I don't think I've had the pleasure—"

"I read one of your letters, Mr. Watson, the one that spoke of your coming."

"So, she knows then?"

"Well, yes, but—"

And for the first time that morning, Henry allowed himself to truly hope. "Then she is not lost. She's waiting for me. Thank you for your time, madam."

Henry turned and marched toward the carriage, Toby swift on his heel. "What are you going to do, sir?"

"*We*, my good man, are going to search for Agnes Archibald."

Chapter 17

In the cool of the afternoon, Agnes had finished chopping a fresh tree down for lumber when Cherry arrived from town. Her face was strained as she carried her basket up the side of the mountain.

"Here, let me help you with that." Agnes rushed to the woman's side.

"Never mind all that, Archie. Come inside before someone sees ye."

"What do you mean?"

Cherry quickened her pace and closed the door behind them, before producing a piece of paper with Agnes' likeness upon it. "There's a reward for ye."

Agnes' brows leapt. "How could they even conjure such a likeness?"

"Notes, perhaps? They're forever taking down descriptions to identify us."

She gazed down into her own faintly sketched face. "I don't understand. Why would Cascades offer a reward for a convicted criminal? Don't they have better things to spend their money on. Like torture chambers..."

"I'm sorry, Archie, but ye'll have to move on," she said softly. "I can't risk someone coming here. I can't risk someone knowing about Mr. Richards."

Agnes opened her mouth to defend herself but part of her knew she was on borrowed time as it was. "Of course, Cherry. I'll leave at nightfall."

Cherry went to stoke the stove's fire. "Where will ye go?"

"The only place I can go," she whispered, "I'll return to Cascades. At least then I might find some employment." She shrugged. "And I can serve off my time." Then, an idea struck her. "And you can deliver me, Cherry."

"Whatever do ye mean?"

"To repay your kindness, you can retrieve the reward."

"I don't know, Archie. That doesn't sound right. It doesn't sound decent."

"Cherry, I'm offering to go back one way or another, you might as well profit from it."

She sighed long and hard. "If ye insist, but I will keep a portion of it aside for when yer free, understand? Ye come and find me when yer a free woman again."

"I shall, you have my word."

"Well, good then. One last cuppa before we go, then?"

Agnes studied the condemning portrait while Cherry made the tea. "It says here you have to deliver me to an address in town."

"Not straight to Cascades then?"

"No, perhaps it's some sort of in between house to process the reward. I can't imagine the matron writing cheques for this sort of thing."

"It's all very strange." Cherry shook her head. "I'll miss ye "round here, Archie."

Agnes cradled the tin cup in her hands and took slow sips, anything to savor this moment before she returned to ox head soup.

❦

Nothing could have prepared Henry for the response to his reward advertisement. Every girl in town—whether she resembled the portrait or not—was brought to his doorstep claiming to be the elusive #227. Toby was their first point of contact at which point he would ask to see their tin ticket. Once they failed the initial test—with each woman claiming to have conveniently lost or misplaced it—they were given one chance to provide their name. Or rather, Agnes' name. Once again, none answered correctly until a young woman with wild red hair asked to speak to Mr. Watson in regard to the subject of his advertisement, a Miss Agnes Archibald.

Henry flung his study doors open, having listened to every word. "Won't you come in, miss—"

"My name is Bridget, I was a friend of Agnes'."

Henry sunk into the high-backed chair behind his desk and gestured to the one opposite. "Was?"

"The day Mr. Tucker died, God rest his soul, I went to warn Agnes. I overheard my master talking with the boys, saying they were gonna grab her in the night."

Fury burned down Henry's limbs and crawled up his spine.

"That was the last I saw of her. Headed into the woods, I reckon." She picked up a copy of the reward poster. "With all due respect, she won't come back for this, sir. Not when she doesn't know who she's comin' to."

"Toby." Henry stood and pulled on his coat. "Please see Miss Bridget to the door, then pack some supplies. We are heading up the mountain." He opened his drawer and retrieved a pouch of gold coins then placed it on the desk before the young woman. "Thank you for taking the time to come today, Miss Bridget, it is most appreciated. You are a good friend."

"I pray ye find her, sir." Bridget tentatively took the pouch then bobbed a small bow and followed Toby to the front door.

Henry scraped a hand over his after-five shadow. According to Toby, Mr. Tucker had passed away weeks ago, which mean Agnes had been alone in the forest all this time. With the strange summer that was unfolding, with heavy rains and hailstorms, he prayed he would find her unharmed.

Chapter 18

In the misty twilight, Agnes and Cherry started their journey down the mountain in hopes of remaining unseen till they arrived at their destination. Sharp cold rain pelted with the wind against them, Agnes kept her eyes on the ground before her, hat down, coat collar up around her neck. She'd known summers in England more pleasant than this one. Her trusty boots slipped in the mud, sending her tumbling paces ahead of Cherry who shuffled after her.

"Whose idea was this again?" Cherry muttered, helping Agnes to her feet.

"Mine apparently." She smoothed down her coat then paused mid-motion. "Sshh."

Agnes closed her eyes and listened to the forest, the distant waterfall, the river stirring, the rain beating against the trees. The marsupials scattering from the burrows under the cover of the dark. Then, somewhere to the south-east, footsteps squelching in the mud. Two pairs as far as she could tell. She skirted around the trunk of a tall gum and pressed up against it. Cherry tucked behind a native bushel.

Voices travelled on the bitter wind, one man talking far more than the other. He sounded young and boisterous, yet polite all at once. Agnes cringed. She was sure that politeness would be lost the moment he discovered them and the fact that she was a young woman. She may have been scrawny now, with little feminine appeal, but she knew that didn't matter to the men in Van Diemen's Land. All they wanted was an easy picking.

She wrapped her slick hands around the axe handle and braced herself. If they came any closer, so help her she'd break one of them, or both if they tried anything. There mightn't be much to her, but between the wood chopping and Cherry's baking, she at least had strength enough in her arms to put up a good fight.

"Please, God," she whispered in her heart. "Please protect us."

"Hey, you! Sir, I have a question," the young man approached through the thick of the foliage.

Agnes glanced up at the darkening skies. God, help her.

"Hey," he called again, louder.

She stepped out from the shadow of the tree and kept her head down.

"Hey, we're looking for a lass about eighteen. Grey-eyes. Brown curly hair. You seen her?"

"Not "round here," Agnes said gruffly, trying to deepen her voice.

The young man sighed. "Well, I don't suppose you have a place my master and I can wait out this storm?"

Agnes shook her head, and trudged down the mountain, trying to lead him as far away from her hidden friend as possible.

He scampered after her, sliding down the mud and finding his feet. "We just need some shelter is all. We don't mean no harm. You're the first person we've—"

She heard him slip and fall with a thump and cry out in pain.

Agnes quickened her pace, but the second man approached from her right, striding toward her in a wide hat and large overcoat. Her feet fell into frantic stumbling, but his own traversing of the slick mountainside seemed sure and steady.

"Excuse me, sir," he began, his voice far more commanding than the first, "Have you seen—"

His hand grasped her forearm. She turned, panting, axe at the ready.

"Don't touch me!" she shrieked. "So help me, I'll—"

His hand released her in an instant.

Agnes' grip on the axe handle went flaccid as she gazed into the ocean eyes from four hundred moons ago.

"Henry?"

∽

Henry was not sure what he had expected to find, but Agnes Archibald in men's clothes wielding an axe had not entered his wildest imaginations.

He raised his hands as though she might still come at him. "Yes, Agnes," he began gently, squinting through the rain at the woman who had long bewitched him. "Yes, it's me."

Without hesitation, she tossed the axe aside and fell into his arms. Her hands gripped his coat and she melted into his larger frame as though she'd always belonged there. His arms instinctively enfolded her, determined never to let go. Then his hand reached up under her hat, into the hair he had so long wanted to touch. Every societal wall between them crumbled. Here in Van Diemen's Land, they simply did not exist.

"Thank you, Lord," he whispered, and placed a brief kiss upon her weathered hat.

She tipped her head back and he gazed into those grey eyes. "That's rather untoward of you, Mr. Watson." Her lips twitched. Oh, how he wanted to claim them for his own.

"Well, I suppose this must be the man ye've spoken so highly of." Cherry staggered down the mountain toward them. "Ye all just come on up to the cabin, it's simple but it's warm. Or ye'll catch your death."

Henry wrapped his arm around Agnes' shoulders and followed the elderly woman back up the hill.

"Uh, a little help here, sir," Toby groaned, nursing his ankle in the mud.

Henry sighed. "Now what have you gone and done?"

With Agnes by his side, they eased their way over the protruding tree roots to reach Toby in his distress.

"Allow me," Cherry said, appearing at the boy's side. "I'm stronger than I look. Leave the two of "em be."

Toby moaned as Cherry helped him to his feet then proved to be the ideal height for his crutch. Once on his feet, he nodded to Agnes. "You must be the famous Miss Archibald."

"I am."

"Mr. Watson's come a long way to find you, ma'am."

She peered up into Henry's face with a look he'd never seen before. "I dare say he has."

The round effervescent woman led the way back up the mountain till they reached a hidden cottage by the river. Henry could see the piles of wood testifying to Agnes' efforts. Despite her hard work and hard hands, she looked surprisingly well. Her eyes were bright, even if her face proved a little thin. He would do anything to make sure she was looked after and thriving. Even more so than her time at Mildred's Court, because now he had the freedom to just be Henry. Although, there was one mountain he wasn't sure they had yet overcome.

"What about your sentence?"

"I was about to turn myself in when you found me just now." She stole a glance at Cherry in the kitchen, then to Toby reclining on the settee.

"Oh, he's the trustworthy sort." Henry nodded in Toby's direction before taking hold of Agnes' calloused hands.

"Well, there's some sort of warrant for me, a reward to turn me in."

"Yes, I know, I orchestrated it."

"You what?"

"I had to find you. Cascades said you were missing and as good as dead, but I couldn't believe that, and I knew that if someone in town had you then they would be tempted with a reward. Then your friend Bridget came and said you'd likely gone into the woods."

She nodded slowly as understanding dawned.

He watched her for a long moment. "Please say something."

"I can't go back to Cascades," she whispered.

"I'm not saying you should."

"But you think I should serve out my sentence?"

"Well, what about your friend here, what does she think?"

Cherry had set the tea down and opened her mouth to speak, when Agnes interrupted.

"Don't involve her. She has nothing to do with this."

Henry squeezed her hand. "Agnes, you seem to forget that I am on your side."

She visibly relaxed and placed her other hand atop his. "I know, I'm sorry. But after not knowing who to trust for so long..." She shook her head. "I just don't know."

"Agnes," he began softly, "it has been a long day. Let's sleep on it and talk about it in the morning. Once this miserable storm has passed."

She let out a breathy laugh and took a sip of tea. "So much for those hot Australian summers we were promised."

Chapter 19

In the dead of night, while this strange new world slept, Henry tossed and turned in the armchair. Toby's snore from the settee only escalated his frustration, until he remembered Agnes too was sleeping in the adjoining room. The thought of her being so close and yet so far, brought a familiar warmth to his middle. She was here, for now, but what of her sentence? What if someone learned of her being here?

Despite the darkness, he reached into his waistcoat pocket and drew out the portrait. How strange it was of another woman entirely but now he only saw Agnes.

He snapped it shut, returned it to the place by his chest, and strode toward the front door. Conflicting emotions fought against his better judgement. In the eyes of the laws of man, Agnes Archibald was a convict who ought to serve out her seven-year sentence. In the eyes of Henry Watson, however, Agnes Archibald was falsely accused. Yes, she had a criminal past but that was over with, it was over the moment he had offered her honest employment and she had heartily and gratefully accepted. Her dedicated work ethic only further proved what sort of woman she truly was, for a thief by nature would certainly take advantage of such a position—not Agnes. Her gratitude shone in her work and with every passing day, as he watched her from afar, he knew she was the woman he wanted by his side.

He paced the length of the wood-planked porched and leaned against the rail, gazing up at the sky. The rain had finally cleared and in the cloudless sky he saw a vast constellation of new stars. Rarely had he paused to look up at the heavens—in London they could scarcely be found—but here, in this foreign world, the wonder of Creation overwhelmed him with a strange new force. God created the heavens and the earth, male and female, He created them. This world reflected His glory, His beauty, and as children of God, they reflected His likeness.

Agnes reflected His likeness.

He gazed up at the moon, the same moon that hung on the other side of the equator graced this southern sky. And as he reflected upon the goodness of God bringing him so far and for helping him find the woman God himself had thrown in his path that November, he remembered the last time he had been lost in the wonder of the Lord. When the sun was rising over the horizon, over the *William Metcalfe*, over God's own words on the page... *"Therefore if any man be in Christ, he is a new creature: old things are passed away; behold all things are become new."*

"All things," Henry whispered.

In the stillness of the night, with the whisper of marsupials scurrying the ground and the gentle stirring of the river, a supernatural peace descended upon him. Clarity pierced his mind and his heart until no conflict could be found. Henry knew what he had to do, what he had been called to do that November when he first gazed into the grey eyes of Agnes Archibald. He was born to protect that woman. His childhood trauma only made sense in light of God's plan for him and Agnes, and the Lord was using Henry's own past to give him the grace he needed to love her.

He didn't have to try and work it all out, he just had to trust. God had hold of him, and He had hold of Agnes. This was part of His divine plan.

"You couldn't sleep either?" Agnes asked from the front door.

He turned and watched her pull the blanket closer around her shoulders. "You're cold." He went to her, his hands rubbing her arms to warm them.

"What are you doing out here?"

"Thinking. Praying."

"And what conclusion have you come to?"

His hands slowed until they held her arms secure. "We have to run."

Slowly, she began to nod. "We need to leave now, don't we?"

"I know you don't want to involve Cherry any more than you need to."

Her head hung and she gave it a swift shake.

"And Toby will look after her. He's a good lad."

She peered up at him. "Can he chop wood?"

He chuckled. "Can he chop wood... Yes, Agnes, he can, and he can also make an incredible cup of tea."

"They'll get along just fine then. Cherry will enjoy having someone to mother. I'll go write a note."

But as she turned, he took hold of her hand. "Agnes," he began softly, "you don't have to do this if you don't want to."

"Says the man risking everything to rescue me." She gazed up at him. "Henry, I already knew I would follow you anywhere. I just never imagined you felt the same way."

His chest constricted and he had to wonder whether he had the self-control to be alone with this woman. Who was he fooling, he knew the answer. There was only one thing to be done.

"Will you marry me?"

Her mouth fell open and she stood frozen. "Pardon?"

"Will you marry me, Agnes?"

"But how? Who would even—"

"Agnes Archibald." He chuckled, shaking his head. "I asked you a question."

The blanket tumbled from around her shoulders, and she fell into him, face pressed into his chest. "Yes! Yes, a thousand times over."

He smoothed her hair and kissed it. "Go get dressed and write your note, then we'll leave."

✍

Agnes was never the sort of girl who dreamed of her wedding day, but even her wildest of imaginings couldn't have prepared her for this. Beneath the veil of dusk, Henry awoke the priest of St David's to officiate their ceremony. His wife and daughter acted as witnesses and before God, with a getaway horse tied to the front gate, Henry spoke the words she'd never thought she would hear, vowing to love her till death did them part.

Agnes repeated the vows while drinking in those immense ocean eyes. She had hoped for a dress at least, perhaps some flowers. Instead, she was dressed in men's trousers, an oversized shirt and suspenders. She could only laugh at the ridiculousness of it. Henry Watson of Mildred's Court was standing in a convict-built church in Van Diemen's Land pledging himself to a woman on the wrong side of the law.

Once they had left Cherry's cottage and made their way down the mountainside, Henry had thought to collect a few supplies from his townhouse along with the horse Toby had organized upon his arrival. One of the heaviest items was his Bible that had travelled with him from England, and evidently, he wasn't about to leave it behind and strapped it securely to the saddle.

Agnes figured if there was anyone they could trust in town, it would be a priest and his family. Though was certain even if he proved insincere and went to the authorities, they would have put leagues between them and the town before the sheriff could pursue them.

From deep within his pocket, Henry produced a simple ring. He smiled at it first, like it held a hidden secret, then whispered, "I had it made from the token you gave me."

Agnes' breath caught in her chest as she saw the faint markings of two hearts wrapped around the edge of the ring.

"I don't know how they did it, but the year is inside." He angled it to show her the 1835 marked clearly within before he slid it on her fourth finger.

"You had this made back in England?"

"Of course."

"You knew... you knew then..."

"Agnes," he breathed. "I've always known."

Tears streamed down her cheeks and without another word from the priest, she leapt up on tiptoe to claim Henry's mouth with her own. Her arms wrapped around his neck, pulling her into him, and he responded eagerly, chasing her so her feet fell flat once more. Then, breathless, she tore herself away.

"Well," the priest said, "I now pronounce you husband and wife. You may kiss your bride, sir. Again."

Henry grinned and he leaned in to tenderly brush her lips with his. His kiss was far more polite than hers had been but she could sense the desire in his self-control.

"Thank you, Father." Henry nodded to the priest before sweeping Agnes up in his arms. "Now we really must go."

Chapter 20

It would be three days' ride from Hobart Town to Southport, where Henry hoped they could find a willing captain to take them to the mainland.

With the wind at their backs, chestnut curls escaped from beneath Agnes' hat and whipped across his line of sight as he drove the mare forward. His wife was nestled behind him in the saddle, her arms wrapped around his abdomen, her chest pressed into his back. It was enough to drive a man senseless, but he attempted to focus on the task at hand—put as much distance between them and Hobart Town as possible. He could only hope they were both presumed dead, Agnes by running away, and he after going in search of her. He couldn't risk either of them being recognized.

Silent prayers remained on his lips and his heart the whole ride until the moon rose in its full glory and exhaustion slowed them down. He tugged on the reins, alerting a dozing Agnes who slumped into his back.

"I must have fallen asleep..."

"We'll rest here for the night." Henry dismounted the horse and looked around before helping Agnes from the horse. Without hesitation, she took the horse by the reins and led him to a nearby brook for a drink. She then splashed her own face and washed her neck.

Henry kept his attention on the dark spaces between the trees, waiting for an animal or a native to emerge from the stillness, but in all his waiting, nothing came except for the hum of insects.

After a few minutes, he opened the saddlebag to find bread and cheese, and carrots for the horse. He hadn't had the chance to name her since his arrival but figured he would leave the task to Agnes. Tearing the bread and cheese, he placed some in her lap then folded his hands and gave thanks for the meal.

"Not exactly potted-beef and buttery toast, is it?" she asked with a hint of a smile.

"You remember?"

"I remember you smiling as you prayed after I'd remove the lid."

He nodded, chuckling. "I'm afraid salted porridge just didn't compare on those other mornings."

"One day," Agnes began wistfully, "I'll make you your favorite meals every day."

He took her hand and kissed it. "One day, Agnes, you'll be beside me at a fine table and we shall have someone to cook them for both of us."

"You still haven't told me all that happened. What of your business and your home in Mildred's Court?"

"I sold it all." He shrugged and took a wide bite of cheese then swallowed. "And that money went a long way to buy a townhouse here, a man to manage it, and all that. I still have plenty left over."

She nodded. "I'm afraid I bring nothing more to this arrangement than the clothes on my back."

"My dear Agnes." His gaze fixed on hers. "You have no idea how much you have to offer a man, and it far outweighs all the money in the world."

"Whatever it is, it's all yours."

His insides twisted beneath her words and tension rose, warming him from the inside out. "Agnes—"

She leaned closer from upon the strewn log until she was but a breath away, then her soft mouth pressed against his.

It surprised him at first, her assertiveness, yet simultaneously thrilled him. He didn't want a wife who was all politeness and stood on ceremony about such things. The fact that she desired him as he did her caused his heart to stir into utter chaos.

With her mouth pressed against his, she reached for the buttons of his waistcoat, and it was the permission he needed to smooth the suspenders from her shoulders.

Agnes squealed with delight as they tumbled back into the leaves, her landing upon him, pinning him to the ground. And there beneath the Australian starlight, Henry and Agnes found each other and lost themselves in wonder.

⚮

A shiver crept over Agnes' body as she lay naked beneath their coats, save for the tin ticket that still hung around her neck. Tangled in Henry's limbs, her core was warm though her exposed arms were covered in gooseflesh. She was about to wriggle her way free in hopes to clothe herself when her attention was seized by a native woman, also naked, searching their belongings that lay haphazardly strewn over rocks and bushes. Agnes blushed at the sight of it, a mess of hers and Henry's clothes they hadn't been able to take off quick enough.

The native woman peered up at her curiously, then touched her own neck. She wore a necklace of threaded hair.

Agnes touched her own red ribbon with its piece of tin and the native woman backed away, leaving their things upon the ground, and disappearing into the foliage. Agnes lurched to sit upright. "Wait—"

She knew the woman likely wouldn't understand, but she hadn't expected a woman of the land to create a connection between the two of them. Somehow, because she too wore something around her neck, and she too was bare skinned, the woman peaceably just went on her way.

"What's the matter," Henry muttered, reaching across to draw her back into their cocoon.

"I saw a native woman," Agnes said. "She was... lovely."

His brow creased. "I've only heard stories of them being aggressive."

She shook her head. "So have I, but she was only curious. Wait, she's coming back."

"Is she..."

"Naked? Yes."

Henry closed his eyes and feigned sleep.

The native woman appeared from between the great eucalyptus trees, a heavy beast upon her shoulders. She kneeled beneath the weight and dumped the kangaroo at their feet. Agnes felt Henry jolt beside her. The woman grunted toward the creature and spoke in another language.

Agnes pulled the coat to cover herself and placed a hand on her chest. "For us?"

The native woman continued to speak in another language, gesturing to the kangaroo and then to some sticks. Then, with a final word Agnes couldn't understand, she vanished once more into the landscape.

"Dare I ask what's laying on my bare feet."

"Why, husband, it's a dead kangaroo, of course."

Henry's feet recoiled from beneath the beast and he sat erect in their makeshift bed. "Well, would you look at that. Breakfast."

"Come on, let's get dressed and then I'll try to work out how to cook this thing."

"I'm afraid I'll make a poor assistant," Henry admitted, watching her clamber for her clothes.

"I think this ones yours." She giggled, trying to sort through the various men's clothes strewn around them. She fiddled with the waistcoat approvingly, distinctly recalling the moment she had been so bold to try to remove it from her husband, when a gold case fell out. Curious, she picked it up and fingered the filagree pattern before opening it. Every warm feeling from the night before fell away. "Who is this?"

"You, of course." Henry's cheeks flushed. "I mean, it's not, but don't you think she rather looks like you. Just look at the eyes, the hair..."

"Henry, I asked you a question. Who the hell is this in the portrait?"

She watched the Adam's apple bounce in his throat and his face drained white. "Well, I mean, technically, I suppose, it's Josephine, but when I found it in my drawer—"

"You've kept her portrait all this time?"

"My father's things were kept in my office drawer. I'd forgotten about it when you arrived—"

"You decided to keep it on your person?"

"Agnes, I understand how this must look, but I didn't have a portrait of you and—"

"So you've had a portrait of another woman with you. Why? Are you still in love with her?"

"What? Agnes, no. It was to help me find you. You must admit the resemblance is—"

Agnes pulled her clothes to cover herself. "That woman is not me!" She felt the pain of her heart strike her face as realization dawned. "Or is she..."

"Whatever do you mean?"

"Was Mrs. Green right all along?"

"Agnes, don't be ridiculous."

"Ridiculous? Me? I'm not the one harboring feelings for someone I knew when I was twelve."

"I'm not—" He exhaled loudly. "If you'd just let me explain..."

"So you can tell me more lies? I don't think so."

And before he could respond, Agnes ran into the woods.

Chapter 21

In the blazing of the dawn, Agnes tumbled through the foliage, pulling on her clothes as she went. Thin grey branches whipped against her body, and she ignored every sensible thought that told her to turn back. She had been utterly wrong about Henry Watson. He was just like the rest of them. Only instead of using brute force, Henry had the audacity to make her fall in love with him first before he had his way with her. Now he had taken what he wanted—a substitute for his long-lost Josephine—he would likely disappear.

She staggered over the rocky surface, Henry's beckoning call became more distant with her every step. There was no way he would risk bringing his precious horse over such terrain. Agnes shook her head and her tears swept up with the wind. When the forest finally thinned, she was overwhelmed by the scent of the ocean. She followed it, followed the call of the waves through the last of the ferns to the rocky edges that led to white sand. She had reached the shoreline, but she wasn't alone.

A vessel was anchored a short way offshore and its crew washed in the sea. Agnes came to an abrupt halt on the sand. A whistle from one of the men alerted the others till they waded through the shallow waters toward her. She swallowed the lump rising in her throat but just as she thought to run, one of the men seized her hand.

"Going so soon?" he asked, yanking her further onto the sand.

"Pretty little thing," another remarked, smoothing her cheek. She turned and spat at him, turning his expression from one of admiration to pure hatred. "Why you little—" His calloused hands took hold of her. "Right men, for that I get to go first."

"Like hell you are, I saw her first," said the other.

Another threw his hat into the ring and pulled her by the waist. "Let me see if she's any good before ye have a go."

Uncontrollable tears rolled down Agnes' face as she writhed against the man. The other snickered, watching as he pushed her into the sand. She screamed. His hand went to her mouth. She bit down hard. He recoiled only to grab a fistful of hair and force her head back into the sand. He fought against her trousers. Agnes kicked and screamed till two other men came to hold her down. This was it. Blood rushed to her head. She was going to pass out. This was going to happen. What she'd swore she would never allow—

Just as the man was about to have his way, a bullet pierced the air, halting every muscle in his body.

Henry appeared through the foliage, high upon horseback, pistol level and pointed at the man straddling her.

Agnes' desperate eyes fixed on him.

His chin trembled but his glare proved fierce. "Unhand my wife!"

❧

Henry could have killed them all in that moment and he doubted he would've felt the least bit guilty. The thought of those men touching Agnes made him sick to his core.

He dismounted the horse, keeping the pistol he had hoped he'd never have to use level and pointed square at the man who now scrambled across the sand away from Agnes. Not taking his eyes from him, Henry leaned down, took Agnes' upper arm, and lifted her into his side. With her curled against his chest, he cocked the gun with his thumb.

"Now, now," a man called from the launch boat on the water, "that won't be necessary!"

The sailors backed away, a couple of them even turning to help the launch boat straight onto the sandy shore. Three women sat with the middle-aged man, one his own age, and two others far younger.

"That is no way to treat a potential customer, *être parti!*" He eyed the men with disgust. "Forgive them, madam, I hope they did not harm you."

Henry could feel Agnes trembling at his side, but she didn't utter a word.

"I am Monsieur Moreau, this is my wife and our two daughters." Monsieur Moreau waded through the last of the shallows and presented himself to them with open hands. "Believe me, we mean you no harm. I am a *merchande.*"

Henry uncocked the pistol and lowered the weapon.

Agnes glared up at him. "What are you doing? They're pirates!"

He tried not to meet those eyes lest she undo him completely. He was as disheveled as she with his shirt barely buttoned, but he knew that if he lingered upon her he would forget all the frustration and anger that had just coursed through his body at her running away so foolishly, quarrel or not. "They're not pirates," he said softly, "they're merchants."

"Oh."

"Now, please Agnes, climb upon the horse."

"Why, where are you going?"

"There's something I need to do." He didn't wait to see if she had done as he asked but he marched past the merchant and his family. He took the gold-encased portrait from his pocket, squeezed it in his fist until it started to pinch, then hurled it into the ocean. Then, without a word, he nodded to the merchant and strode back to the horse. Mounting it, he eyed Agnes expectantly as she stood defiant on the sand. "Are you coming?"

She nodded once and climbed up behind him.

"Good day to you," Henry called to the merchant, then clambered up the hill with his bride, fighting every urge to scold her like a child. He had heard it countless times from the pulpit that men ought to love their wives as Christ loved the church. Well, look how that turned out, the church did far worse than Agnes had done today, and Christ still died for them and offered them eternal life. The least Henry could do was wait until his anger subsided until they addressed the situation with love. And if he was truly honest with himself, he wasn't sure how long he could even stay angry at his beautiful headstrong wife.

Chapter 22

Agnes' second night as a married woman proved sweetly silent. Henry held her as she drifted to sleep in the nook beneath his arm and he did not speak a word of the happenings of the morning other than to remind her once again how beautiful she was before he began to softly snore.

By the third day, they were nearing their destination when Henry guided the horse off track to admire the great caves that lay inland. Tying the horse to a tree outside, he took Agnes' hand and led her within. It was warmer than the air beyond, and the sound of trickling water echoed through the vast cavern. Sunlight filtered through the trees beyond the mouth of the cave and glistened on the steamy surface of the water.

Henry peered back at her. "I have heard of these—thermal springs."

Agnes' curious expression brightened. "Like an enormous bath?"

He chuckled and began to remove his coat. "I suppose so."

"What are you doing?"

"What do you think?" He was already down to his trousers. "I'm taking a bath."

Agnes' mouth gaped as her husband unashamedly undressed before her. Certainly, she had seen him before, but it had been dark and in a moment of passion. She'd barely paused to take him in at all. Now, she found herself embarrassed.

He stepped into the water before sinking all the way in. "Oh, Agnes, it's incredible, come in."

She shyly fingered the front of her shirt. One by one, she unbuttoned herself and began to remove the men's clothes that swallowed her femininity. "I might keep my shift on."

"Of course." He floated back, relishing in the water.

Agnes piled her things together on the rocks before dipping her toes into the edge. Steam rose in clouds around her. The water was temptingly warm.

"Do you have spare under clothes in the saddlebag?" Henry asked.

She shook her head once and his countenance shifted to one of amusement. Then he swirled around in the water, keeping his back to her.

"Go on and take it off, I won't look."

"Promise?"

"I mean, you are my wife, but of course I promise. I won't do anything you aren't comfortable with, Agnes."

She exhaled in relief and took off the final pieces of clothing before rushing into the water and bobbing down so only her shoulders were above the surface.

"May I turn around now?"

"You may."

The broadest grin she'd ever seen spread across his face and he swam toward her till he lingered a foot before her. "May I have permission to kiss you, Mrs. Watson?"

A trembling laugh escaped her. "You may, Mr. Watson."

He leaned in, cupped her face with one hand, and pressed a sweet kiss to her mouth. "There now," he whispered, "that's all I'll take, I promise."

Her insides quaked and she wasn't sure if it was the kiss or the fact that she felt entirely safe. "Henry, I am sorry about yesterday."

"As am I."

"I know it was foolish of me to run."

His neck visibly flushed, and he shook his head. "I don't want to think of what might have happened if the horse had slipped a shoe, if I couldn't find you..."

"Well, Monsieur Moreau—"

"Was alerted when I sounded the gun," he stated plainly.

Her cheeks warmed. "It's just... when I saw that portrait I... I felt like all my fears were becoming reality. I thought I'd been used in the worst way and I just had to get away. I just had to."

"I know what it looked like but believe me, it was never that way. I didn't even know what love was as a boy. I'd certainly never witnessed it between my parents. But now that I have... I don't want to lose it."

She sighed. "I am sorry."

"I know. Just, please, no matter what stupid thing I do, please don't leave me."

Agnes bit down on her lip. Hard. She needed the sting of pain to counter her rising tears. "I wasn't leaving you, I just... I needed a moment."

"I don't want to lose you, Agnes. It happened before and I don't want it to happen again. I don't think I could bare it."

Sincerity burned in his gaze and she closed the space between them, wrapping her wet arms around him. She buried her face into his neck and breathed him in. "Henry, I had no idea—"

"No idea I have fallen so deeply in love with you, I would chase you across oceans and gladly shoot down any man who dares to touch you."

A small gasp escaped her lips and she couldn't let him go. Her arms tightened around him, and she threaded her fingers into his hair. "I love you, Henry."

She felt his body tremor with a suppressed sob and so she held onto him. Beneath the jagged rocks of the cavern above, tears seeped into the fresh springs that held them, washing away the past and clearing the way for a brave new future. Together.

❧

When Henry led Agnes from the caves that afternoon, the mare was nowhere in sight.

"Blast!" He shook his head, cursing himself, before turning his attention to the overcast sky. "Lord, where is that blasted horse?" Then, silently, he repented for taking such a tone with the Lord God Almighty.

Agnes paced the space outside the caves. He knew what she was thinking, they had wasted time, they had been foolish to stop for so long. Perhaps he hadn't tied the horse as securely as he thought, though she was rarely one to run away. Perhaps something spooked her? Perhaps she'd been stolen?

"Here," Agnes began, "that's a horse track there. And another here."

He peered over at her. "Pardon?"

"Have you ever tried following rabbits in the woods, they're so fast. You need to find where they're hiding and wait for them to come out, that's when you take your shot."

"I'm not following. How do you even know this?"

"Farmer's daughter with a partiality for rabbit stew over plain vegetables," she said as though that explained everything. "Come on, follow me." Agnes studied the ground she walked upon, flinging back branches, and stumbling over logs. "I'd say she got spooked by something. Her prints are a bit erratic. Maybe one of those giant googly eyed birds? They're sure to scare the life out of anyone."

"Emus." Henry nodded as he followed. "Yes, they are strange creatures."

Agnes came to an abrupt halt and raised her hand. "There, in the clearing."

To be sure, the mare and all their belongings with her were in a small meadow scented with eucalyptus with native wildflowers rising around her hooves. A creek trickled and coursed its way through some slick moss-covered rocks and the horse leaned low to drink.

"Stay here." Agnes crept slowly toward the mare. With both hands raised, she hushed gently. The mare whinnied again, raising her head. Agnes slowed her approach. "It's alright, lovely one. You're safe."

From across the way, a mirror-like image stared back at them. A wild caramel-colored horse rose up on her hind legs then disappeared into the woods once again. Agnes slowly approached the mare and took its head in her hands, stroking her gently. "Is that who startled you, girl?" she whispered so softly it was barely audible. "A wild horse?"

"I dare say it was what they call a Brumby," Henry said quietly, drawing closer.

Agnes continued to stroke the mare's face. "Perhaps that's what we should call you? You need a name. What about Brumby?"

"You do know she's a girl."

"Of course, I do. What's wrong with the name Brumby for a girl? It's a good strong name."

Henry chuckled. "Yes, I am sure you're right, Mrs. Watson. Brumby it is."

Agnes threw a playful look over her shoulder. "Why do I get the feeling you're going to call me 'Mrs. Watson' any time you're indulging me?"

"Well, I best call you Mrs. Watson all the time then, Mrs. Watson." He drew closer until he could smell the sweet scent of her. "Because I have every intention of indulging you as often as I can."

"Be careful, Mr. Watson, a girl could get used to that."

Chapter 23

By the time the sun began to set over Van Diemen's Land, Agnes and Henry reached the shores of Southport. Its turquoise water turned gold beneath the shifting sky and Agnes followed Henry to the wharf on foot, leading Brumby along by the reins.

"Stay here and keep your head down," Henry told her gently, coming to a halt under a gumtree a short way off from the water. "I will enquire about transport to the mainland."

Agnes kept her wide brim over her face and nodded.

He crouched a little to look her in the eye. "Mrs. Watson," he whispered. "I love you."

Her lips tugged into a smile. "And I love you, Mr. Watson."

"I will only be a moment."

Agnes kept her attention fixed on Henry as he strode down the wharf toward a group of seamen. Her stomach growled after the aroma of grilled fish wafting from the local tavern. She waited by Brumby, certain a decent meal would be their next stop before boarding a vessel.

Heavy footsteps approached. "Miss, remove your hat."

She jolted and tightened her grip on Brumby's reins. From the corner of her eye, she spotted the poster Henry had circulated in the constable's grip, only in messy ink was scrawled, "Missing from Cascades."

The constable stepped forward, peering under the wide brim.

Agnes met his eye, stepping back. "That is not me, sir."

"Like hell it isn't."

He reached for her tin ticket, and she pulled back, forcing the red ribbon to snap. The constable stumbled back.

Mounting Brumby, Agnes kicked her into a gallop.

"Stop that woman!" the constable shouted, running for his own horse, the poster flailing in the wind behind him.

Agnes urged the mare off road and into the woods. She couldn't think, all she knew was that she had to survive.

Trees whipped past as Agnes fought her way through the lush landscape. Horse hooves followed on her trail, shouts echoed through the trees, and she knew she was on borrowed time. She should have known her time was Henry was too good to be true. There was no way she could sail off to the mainland and be a good wife to him. They had only been married a couple days and she had already made a mess of it.

She wrestled the temptation to reach for the pistol she knew was in the saddlebag. She could not bring herself to shoot a man in cold blood, not when in truth he was only doing his job.

So she did what was completely unnatural to her. She stopped fighting. Pulling on the reins, Brumby came to a standstill long enough for the constable to reach them. Agnes raised both hands and held them either side of her head.

"227 you are under arrest." The constable cocked his gun.

"That won't be necessary, sir. I'll come willingly." Slowly, she began to dismount Brumby. "May I simply ask that the horse be returned to my husband, Mr. Henry Watson?"

"You don't make demands of me, you evil wretch."

And with a sharp strike on the back of her head, Agnes' vision failed and she slipped into blackness.

∽

Dread filled Henry the moment the commotion reached him.

"No, Agnes—"

His feet sprinted into a run. He narrowed his gaze in on the constable mounting his horse. Panting, Henry thrust himself forward. His body ached for more than food, it ached for his wife safe in the nook beneath his arm. Now, she was the target of a pursuit and he'd be damned if he allowed anyone to hurt Agnes again. Before he could intervene, they both disappeared into the woods and Henry, on foot and in the shadows of dusk, lost sight of them. Still he ran, listening for the sounds of the horse's hooves. He staggered over jagged rocks. One sliced into his leg. He stumbled a moment, wincing against the sting, but kept fumbling through the trees. If he could just get to them in time, he could protect her. He could keep her safe. He couldn't lose her again. He just couldn't.

"Agnes!"

He slowed as he reached a small clearing where Brumby stood alone grazing. Henry clambered to the animal and checked the saddlebag. His pistol sat securely where he'd left it. Why had Agnes not thought to use it? Even to bide her time until he arrived. Surely, she knew by now he would follow her to the ends of the earth and beyond. Then Henry's gaze strayed upon his Bible, sitting beside the weapon in the saddlebag, unopened since he began his journey with Agnes. He slumped to his knees just as the sky opened. Blood seeped from the wound on his leg, but it didn't matter. Once again, he was too late.

"Lord God," he whispered, squinting up at the greying skies. "Forgive me for thinking I could do this on my own. Please, help me to protect Agnes, the wife You, Father God, have blessed me with. Please help me not to take that blessing for granted but to show my gratitude every day. Please, Father, help me—"

His voice broke away. He hung his head and staggered to his feet. He wouldn't do Agnes any good sitting here wallowing in the mud, he had to go after her. Glancing down at the wound on his leg, he reached for the flask of gin he kept for emergencies and splashed it directly into the wound. He bit back his groan then ripped a strip of fabric from the end of his shirt to use as a makeshift bandage. Henry reached up, steadying himself on the saddle and pulled himself up onto Brumby's back and headed back toward the town of Southport. He returned to the great gumtree where he had last seen Agnes only to find the reward poster he himself had made strewn in the mud. The reward money had been haphazardly smudged out and above it read, 'Missing from Cascades'. Dismounting Brumby, he took the poster and stored it in his bag. Then something red winked at him from the sodden ground. There in the mud lay Agnes' tin ticket, #227. He scooped it up in his palm and hid it within his waistcoat pocket. He prayed one day this ticket would mean nothing, she would not be a number anymore, but Agnes Watson, his beloved, his wife. He prayed one day their lives would truly begin. Then he squared his shoulders and raised his chin. Until then, he would do everything in his power to ensure the future of his prayers became a reality.

"Come on, girl," he muttered to the mare and mounted her once more, "we'll go all night if we have to. Let's find Agnes..."

Chapter 24

When the darkness faded and the evergreen landscape finally came into view, Agnes stirred and awoke to the weight of iron cuffs around her wrists and ankles once again. Her head swayed with the shifting movement, and she struggled to focus on the road before her. Unfamiliar arms wrapped around her small frame, and a deep brown horse trudged on beneath her. Everything felt unfamiliar, even the road she travelled.

"Where am I?"

"No talking," the man commanded. "Not unless you want me to silence you."

Agnes pressed her mouth firmly closed and her eyes glazed with tears she would not let fall. She held her sob in her chest. She could not release it. She held it till she was able to steady her breath and she slowly exhaled. Crying would do no good, it would probably just irritate the man. No, if she was going to survive—and survive was what she had always done best—then she would have to go with the terms set out before her. She could not however silence her stomach that had not eaten since lunch with Henry the day before. Only stale bread and cheese, but she would take it over ox head soup any day. After all, that would be where the constable would be taking her, back to Cascades Female Factory. At least her silence now would be useful practice for the long days to come. She could only imagine the punishment she would face as a runaway convict maid. Perhaps she would learn the secrets behind the yellow Cs stitched upon some of the convict women's shifts.

The constable only loosened his grip on her when reaching for food from his bag. "I'm used to riding through the night," he told her gruffly, "so don't you go getting any ideas."

However, by the second night, he could no longer stifle his yawns, so he yanked her from the horse and tied her to a nearby eucalyptus tree. He paused, lingering over her, his fair hair falling over his tanned brow. A single calloused finger stroked her cheek.

"If I wasn't so bloody tired..."

He shook his head and stalked away. He tied off the horse to a thick bough overshadowing a trickling brook. The constable splashed his face then curled up in the leaves with his coat strewn over his shoulders, a saddlebag as his pillow. Agnes waited till she heard his snore, then she allowed herself to sob. Tears flooded her cheeks. To think only the day before she had been safe in Henry's arms, and now she was to face an unfair sentence for a crime she hadn't committed. God had turned her life around since being on the streets of London, He had made an honest woman out of her. He had sent Henry across the world to rescue her.

Henry.

Surely, he was coming after her. Surely, he would find her before they reached Cascades. She would hold onto hope this time. She would trust that the God who brought her out of the darkest places was still working now, even in this moment.

Agnes looked up at the indigo sky. A vast constellation spread before her, and the full moon hung so low she felt like she could almost touch it. Despite the cuffs on her wrists, she wiggled her fingers as though she could feel it, then she felt that small reminder spin around her fourth finger.

She was Henry Watson's wife. It was a truth she had to hold onto, no matter what came. Whether Henry found her in seven minutes, hours, or in the seventh year of her sentence, she would have to be content with that truth. She would hold onto it and hope with every part of her that the God of truth and grace would return them to one another.

❧

By the second evening on the road, Henry's head grew faint. Despite administering alcohol to his wound, it throbbed and wept with infection. He could not go much further without assistance. A little way off the road, he came upon a halfway house of boarders under the supervision of a Mrs. Farraway.

"We don't take in any men," she said firmly, her face filled with suspicion. She placed her large self in the doorway. "You best be on your way. Only ex-convicts here, and they don't need arousing by the likes of you."

Henry could feel the color drain from his face. "Please, if you could just send for a doctor—"

"There ain't no doctors "round these parts, sir. Best I can do is look at you myself, but you ain't coming in this house. You can go "round to the barn."

"Thank you," he whispered, stumbling toward Brumby.

"You better not be a drunkard." She slammed the door behind her.

Sweat trickled down his brow and he shook his head, holding onto his saddle. "No madam, just... just..."

"What's the matter with you anyway?"

"My... leg..."

She glanced down and let out a shriek. "Goodness, why didn't you say something, man!" Her wide shoulder braced him, and he let some of his weight fall on her. Helping him to the barn, she led Brumby to the hay and Henry collapsed without invitation.

"Take those trousers off," she barked.

"Now, madam, I—"

"Don't you go acting all high and mighty, you've got an infection and a fever by the looks of you, I'm not likely to go falling all over myself over a sick man, am I? Now, take your trousers off or I'll do it."

Henry struggled and did as he was bid.

"There now, that wasn't so bad. I'll get you some blankets and towels soon enough. But first, to deal with this nasty wound."

His eyes rolled back into his head. "What are you going to do?"

"My mama once taught me a trick with infection. I'll just head to the kitchen and I'll be back." She bolted the barn door behind herself and locked it with a key.

Henry groaned and adjusted himself on the hay. The barn was small, narrow, with no other animals and little light. Then he noticed the claw marks on the wooden beams of the door. This was not a barn for animals. It was a prison.

Panic set in and he began to shake uncontrollably. What sort of woman kept female convicts in her house and prisoners in the barn? Or perhaps this was where the convicts were sent as punishment, locked up, starved of basic necessities.

By the time Mrs. Farraway returned, she carried a seemingly heavy pot and a large wooden spoon. "Honey."

"Ho-ney?" he muttered through chattering teeth.

She nodded. She doused the wound with alcohol, much as he had done, but then she layered it thickly with honey. "Rest now. I'll come check on you in the morning."

Once again, she bolted the door behind herself and left him alone in the dark.

Still trembling, he curled up on his side and attempted sleep. He'd be no good to Agnes if he didn't rest and recover. But the moment he closed his eyes, all he could see was Agnes' face and the nightmares began all over again. Her scream echoed through his being. Fear ignited every nerve ending. Adrenalin coursed through him driving him on to search her out. She called for him, begging him to rescue her, but she was always out of reach. Then, suddenly, he was twelve years old again, roaming the streets of London on a wisp of courage. He neared that old hotel, too afraid of what he might find. He rounded the façade and braved the alley where rodents smuggled into the tavern's waste, and half-dressed women hung on the backsteps eyeing him as if he was just like his father. He felt hollow. His heartbeat echoed within the confines of his body, and he wished he could turn back, wished he didn't have to face what was coming next. Then he saw her, a frail terrified girl hunched in the corner of that back alley. Her painted face was streaked with tears. She couldn't have been more than fourteen years old. Chestnut curls hung around her face and storm-grey eyes gazed up at him as if he was the only one who could take her from this place, the only one willing to tell her the truth.

She was a child of God.

She was not a thief.

She deserved better than circumstance and hardship had given her.

A whimper left the girl's lips and her dirt-stained hands reached for him. "Help me—"

Part Three

Chapter 25

MARCH 1837, VAN DIEMEN'S LAND

Henry never came for her. Agnes' hope began to fade the moment she stepped through the high stone walls of Cascades Female Factory and was sent into solitary confinement. She would be punished. Severely. Though nothing could prepare her for when the truth was fully exposed.

Agnes was silently at the washtub scrubbing convict men's clothes, the yellow Cs on her cap, sleeve and petticoat testifying to her rebellion, when the ox head soup threated to rise up her throat. She braced herself on the cold hard stone, breathing in the autumn air, praying it would settle the nauseating spells sweeping through her body. She knew the origins, of course, she had known for weeks, but she could not imagine how it might affect her sentencing were anyone to find out. She was living on borrowed time.

With one final shudder through her, she vomited the contents of her stomach into the washtub. Fellow convict women leapt back in disgust. Again and again, Agnes vomited till all that came up was stomach acid.

Matron approached, her grim expression in a hard line. "227, to the hospital with you. Now. Someone, help her."

It was an order few were willing to obey till a familiar face stepped forward. Shadows of bruises still marked her once pretty face, but Bridget came alongside Agnes and helped her lean on her as they trudged toward the Female Factory hospital.

"Thank you. I didn't know you were here," Agnes whispered.

"Just arrived," she said, equally as soft. "Ran away from me master. This place is kinder than he ever was."

"I'm sorry."

"How far along are ye?"

Agnes wanted to deny it, but she knew it was hopeless. "A couple months, I think. I thought the worst of the sickness was over."

"Don't worry, I lost mine before three months. You probably will too in this place."

Agnes stopped beside her. "But... I don't want to... it's..." She swallowed the lump in her throat and reduced her voice so it was barely audible, "The baby is Henry's."

"And where is he now?" Bridget asked. "Probably dead, or with another woman. Best thing that could happen to ye is to let that bairn go. No one wants to have a wee bairn in Cascades. No one."

Agnes shook her head. "I'll fight to help the baby survive. Whatever it takes."

Bridget hooked her arm around Agnes' middle. "Well, it just might take that too."

The roots of bitterness may have reached deep within her only friend, but Agnes was determined it would not claim her and her baby's life too.

Nurse Tedder eyed her suspiciously when she entered, taking in her pasty complexion, the vomit down the front of her shift dress. "When did the symptoms start?"

Agnes was helped onto one of the stiff stale beds in the hospital, and the moment she was settled, Bridget left without a word. Agnes cleared her throat. "About eight weeks."

Nurse Tedder lowered her voice. "That's how far along you think you are?"

Agnes nodded.

Without another word, Nurse Tedder fetched Agnes a large slice of bread and tea with sugar in it. "This is usually kept for breastfeeding mothers down on Liverpool Street, but it looks like you could do with some nourishment."

Agnes' mouth salivated over the treat. Her eyes glistened at the kindly nurse. "Thank you, ma'am."

"Rest now. I will tell the matron you are on bed rest for the next four weeks due to your condition." She paused at the door. "I warn you though, once the baby is here safely and weaned, your punishment will be most severe."

"Worse than pulling rope apart in solitary confinement?"

"I'm afraid so, my dear." Nurse Tedder's kind eyes filled with compassion. "A year's hard labor will follow. Six months for adultery, six months for being pregnant."

"But I am wed," Agnes raised her hand to show the simple ring, still amazed that by some miracle the matron had not yet spotted it. "My child is not illegitimate."

Nurse Tedder shrugged. "Unless both the lieutenant governor and Cascades' Superintendent approved the marriage, it is not legally binding."

Horror struck Agnes. "What do you mean?"

"I don't mean to upset you, but neither do I want you to have hope where there is none. I was in your position two years' ago. My 'husband' has moved on and I am still here."

Agnes gulped against the bile rising in her throat. "Henry's not like that."

She shook her head. "They're men, they're all like that."

"What happened to your baby?"

"I visited him on Sundays for a while."

"Why did you stop?" Agnes asked but feared the answer in the same breath.

"Because illness broke out in the house on Liverpool Street. Now he lays in a shallow grave at St David's." The nurse shook her head. "227, the best thing that could happen is for this child to go to heaven before it meets this cruel world. There is nothing for it here."

"There is hope," Agnes offered bravely, clutching her stomach. "There is always hope."

"Pretty thought," Nurse Tedder muttered and withdrew, leaving Agnes alone with her unborn child.

⌘

Unacquainted with hard labor, Henry found his stay with Mrs. Farraway disconcerting to say the least. Once his infection subsided and his wits returned, he discovered Brumby to be missing and the only item from his saddlebag left in his possession to be his Bible. The only times Mrs. Farraway left the main house was to deliver him stew—of what kind, he dared not enquire—and to give him new jobs to do around the yard.

"But what of my horse? When may I have my horse?"

"When your leg is better." She nodded to it. "Look, you're still limping."

Henry wondered if his limp would prove to be a permanent ailment, for as the weeks went on and he heard the madness from what he came to call Farraway House, full mobility of his leg never returned. Though he could scarcely blame its mistress' medicinal honey.

On a sunny autumn day, as he turned over the soil of the vegetable patch to ready for planting, someone new emerged from the house. He always heard voices, of course, but never saw anyone in person other than Mrs. Farraway. She made it clear the house was established for women finding their way out of their convict pasts, or those who had turned to alcoholism within Cascades' walls and needed a place to practice sobriety where they wouldn't be a menace to society.

This particular woman, however, marched toward him as though she had something to prove, madly waving around a piece of paper he couldn't make out. As she approached, he stood to his full height and held the pitchfork in front of his person, lest she get any bold ideas.

"Why do you have a portrait of me?" she demanded, stormy eyes burning into him. There was nothing to her. Between her gaunt face and scrawny physique, he didn't recognize her to be anyone he ought to be in acquaintance with, let alone carry a portrait of. "I asked you a question!" She held up that blasted reward poster the constable had left back in Southport.

"Does Mrs. Farraway know you have been rummaging through my things?"

"Well, they're not yours anymore, are they," she spat. "Now, why do you have this portrait? And why is there a reward?"

"That's not you, it's someone else."

She stepped toward him, her hair fell limp around her browned face, but for that moment he saw a flicker of resemblance. "I know who took the original portrait and I know what he was after, now you better answer me now, or I'll—"

Warmth drained from Henry's face as he took in the gaunt creature before him. "No, it can't be... Josephine?"

"I did my time," she went on. "That Watson man doesn't have no claim on me anymore. He never did. I showed him."

"Miss Josephine," he softened his voice, "it's me, Henry Watson."

Her brows furrowed and a scowl disfigured her countenance. "He's only a boy. You don't know what you're saying. Now I'll tell you once and I'll tell you proper, don't you go telling Mr. Watson where I am. I made a life for myself here in a new country. I don't owe him nothing."

"Miss Josephine, that Mr. Watson is long dead."

"Serve him right, then. I hope that boy of his got it all. He was the only decent thing in that house. Poor boy, didn't deserve the life he had."

Henry swallowed hard. "Whatever do you mean?"

"That man for a father? He was pure evil. No one deserves a father like that. No one."

He watched her tear the paper into tiny pieces and throw them into the breeze. "That's what I think of him. He's nothing and no one to me anymore. He's the dust beneath my feet." Then, she staggered back inside.

Henry stood for a long moment watching the backdoor, wondering if she would make a reappearance, but she did not. He didn't know why Josephine had been sent to Cascades, but he couldn't wait around to find out. No, he had to stop the same madness from taking over his wife. Imprisoned within those tall stone walls would drive anyone mad and Henry could only imagine what Agnes must be suffering now.

When Mrs. Farraway brought him his stew that evening, he was already waiting by the door of the barn.

"Now you best get some food and rest, Henry," she went on. "You won't get your strength back—"

"I won't be sleeping in the barn tonight."

She paused, tray in hand, staring at him blankly. "You can't mean to presume you wish to sleep inside. Let me assure you, the miss who came out today has been properly punished and you won't be seeing her out here."

"I am grateful for your kindness, Mrs. Farraway, but I must go."

She tutted. "How many times must I ask you to call me Jane."

"Mrs. Farraway," he said sternly. "I have repaid your kindness with labor, and now I must leave. I must find my wife. Now where is my horse?"

With an innocent shrug, she held up the bowl of stew.

Henry's hand rushed to his mouth, and he swallowed the disgust rising up his throat. He winced. "You slaughtered my horse?"

"Well, I did save your life, Henry."

He shook his head and took his open Bible from the haybale beside him. "I have to leave."

"Leave in the morning, if you must," she called after him, hitching her skirt with her free hand to follow him down the muddied path. "You haven't even eaten. You will catch your death—"

"Madam, I will take my chances." Henry strode toward the main road and kept on. "Good night to you."

Chapter 26

Night fell upon Van Diemen's Land and the south wind blew an Antarctician chill. Henry's determined pace slowed and the weight of the great book became great indeed as he shifted it from beneath one arm to the other. His leg still ached, causing a natural limp. He wondered if it would ever be right again.

Fear for Agnes' safety and wellbeing was all that forced him to put one foot in front of the other. Unlike her, he was not accustomed to surviving on his own. He was hungry but didn't know the first thing about catching or even cooking food. He was cold yet all he had was the clothes on his back and he didn't know where to find shelter.

Staggering over a rock on the road, his Bible flew out from beneath his arm, crashing on the floor face down. He caught himself with his hands, sharp pebbles grazing his palms, and glared at the book before him. God had sent him here, hadn't He? God had brought Agnes into Henry's life, so why did He keep taking her away?

"Why must this be so difficult?" Henry challenged the darkening sky sweeping with starlight. "I do not understand! If you wish to take my life, do it quickly would you?"

He half expected it to end right there. After all, who in their right mind challenged the God of the universe and complained to Him about their misfortunes when grace and love were supposed to cover all?

"I am at a loss," Henry confessed, his voice rising. "How on earth can I survive out here on my own, on foot no less? Will you not help me?"

Thunder rumbled in the distance and Henry wondered whether his end was coming near. Perhaps the response of Almighty God would be to smite him down and give Agnes to a far more deserving man. But the storm remained in the far-off skies, hovering over his destination of Hobart Town.

He begrudgingly reached for his Bible. "Please, God, help me help her."

He shook his head. Hope seemed like a distant dream, as distant as the thunder. Or perhaps, the distant sound of a carriage traversing the rough road.

Henry jolted and ran toward the sound. Renewed fire fueled him and the pain in his leg seemed to subside as he raced toward the noise coming toward him.

He stopped short as the carriage rounded the corner, almost running into the caramel horse and its lone driver.

"Woah." Henry raised his free hand and backed away while the driver slowed to a halt. "Please, I'm trying to get to Hobart Town."

The driver raised his hat. "I thought as much, sir."

"Toby?" Relief swiftly replaced his shock. "Tobias Woodhouse, what on earth—"

Toby grinned at him and offered his hand. "I'll explain on the way. Come on sir, you look like you could eat a horse."

Henry let out a breathy laugh. "Well, I don't know about that, but a bit of bread and some of that tea of yours would go a long way."

"Bread is in the sack there, sir. I'm afraid you'll have to wait till we get back to Mrs. Richardson's to have a cuppa tea."

Henry rummaged in the sack while Toby made a wide turn with the carriage. "So," Henry said between mouthfuls, forgetting all etiquette, "how did you find me?"

"Well, put that part down to the grace of God, but the reason I knew to look for you was that woman, Bridget. She's had a right 'nough of the world and joined that Flash Mob. I saw her down the pub the other night and she had a tale to tell about everyone in Cascades, including your Miss Archibald."

"She's Mrs. Watson now," Henry added quietly.

"She mentioned that, but apparently none of it's legal if you don't have the right permissions."

Henry's frown deepened. "You mean to say, according to the law—"

"She's still Miss Archibald, sir."

"Well, that won't do at all."

"There's more, sir."

"Go on."

"Apparently, congratulations are in order."

Henry swallowed his mouthful of bread. "But you said the marriage wasn't legal."

"No, it isn't, but a technicality like that doesn't change the fact you're going to be a father."

Henry unceremoniously choked his mouthful up into his hand. "I—I beg your pardon?"

❦

Days melded together in those nauseating weeks till the symptoms all but subsided and all Agnes was left with was a rounding belly and an aching body. Winter shortened the light hours but not the work day and she returned to her regular duties, yellow Cs still adorning her prison garb. She was grateful not to be sentenced to solitary confinement but the reality of an unbearable future haunted her every day. And with those first precious flutters came simultaneous dread—these people would inevitably take her baby.

After chapel one cold evening, as the women returned to their cramped quarters, Bridget bumped into Agnes, startling her.

"Meet at the gate tonight," she muttered.

Agnes watched Bridget disappear in the dim lantern light to climb into her hammock and feign sleep. Agnes knew all too well whom Bridget now associated with, and she had watched her gather her bargaining goods before sneaking out in the middle of the night. Even if Agnes wasn't exhausted from working at the wash basins, she didn't have anything to bribe the guards with. And suppose it was the one time the Flash Mob got caught, Agnes couldn't risk being sent to solitary confinement while she was with child. No, one night's freedom was not worth losing her baby even before the system took him.

She lowered herself into the hammock and smiled. Of course, she didn't know whether it was a boy or a girl, but she had a hunch. She wondered if she should name him after Henry. At least then, their son would always have a connection to his father, even if he was no longer in his life. Or in her life.

"Please Lord," she whispered in her heart, "please reunite us. Please let us be a family."

Tears pricked the corners of her eyes, and she blinked them away. How she wished she and Henry had just travelled inland and built a small hut somewhere to live in. At least she would know how to look after him. At least they would be together.

By the time the last lamp had been snuffed out, the quarters were almost black save the pale moonlight fighting its way through the lonesome barred window nearly two stories high. Agnes wasn't sure how much more of this place she could take, left alone in the darkness again. Here, Bridget no longer cared for Bible passages read aloud. No, Van Diemen's Land had broken her friend it seemed. But it would not break Agnes Watson. No, it would not.

Agnes rolled to her side and laid a hand on her swollen belly, praying over the little one and his future, her eyes firmly shut. A tap on her shoulder forced them to fly open and she saw the faint outline of Bridget sneaking past her hammock. Agnes shook her head. Bridget paused mid-step while other members of the Flash Mob slipped past, each giving her a nudge. Agnes wished she would just follow them and be done with it. Agnes needed her sleep so she could brave another day.

As the last woman filed past, Bridget leaned in close and hissed a sharp whisper into Agnes' ear.

"Henry."

His name was all it took for Agnes to clamber out of the hammock, almost tumbling to the ground had Bridget not caught her. The arms of her friend from long ago held her and Agnes looked up into that familiar face she used to know framed with its wild red hair. Perhaps, there was hope after all.

Chapter 27

Anticipation drove Agnes all the way down the mountain toward Hobart Town till the women arrived at the doors of the Hope and Anchor Tavern, giggling and carrying on, before doubt and insecurity quelled her confidence. She glanced down at her person—she was filthy, swollen, and unkept. She had never wanted Henry to see her like this again, not since that morning on the streets of London when grace had entered her life and it was never the same again. All those months she wondered over the sealed envelopes he had sent, though refused to see him at Newgate Prison. Now, she was about to come face to face with her beloved Henry after living in Cascades Female Factory and being subject to hard labor despite her condition. She could not imagine how unsightly she must look.

The Flash Mob piled in through the tavern doors, causing a raucous among the men, even Bridget had been swallowed by the revelry inside. As the door swung shut on her, she stood there for a long moment battling herself. Henry could be waiting inside and here she was allowing fear to get the better of her.

She took a deep breath and summoned her courage just as the door swung open. Those ocean eyes of his widened and his mouth gaped. Agnes felt like crawling back into the shadows till Henry enveloped her in his arms.

"I can't believe you're really here." He cradled her head in his hand and kissed her hair.

She remained rigid at first, afraid of him touching her and soiling himself, afraid of him smelling her. But when his arms tightened around her, her resolve melted and she reached up and around him and clung to him as though her life depended on it.

"Where were you?" she whispered.

"It's a rather long story, shall we go inside?"

"I'd really rather not." She forced a smile. "Can't we just enjoy the fresh air?"

Despite the winter chill, Henry nodded then removed his coat and draped it around her shoulders. "Shall we take a walk?"

"I'd like that." She took the arm he offered and followed him down the street toward the wharf. At first, Agnes thought the ground uneven, but no, Henry had adopted a slight limp. She longed to ask him of it, but she had so many other questions that came first. The tide caught the moonlight as they ebbed and flowed, and Agnes wrapped her arms about herself.

"Is it true?" Henry asked, stopping alongside her and glancing down.

She nodded and silently took his hand to place it upon her swollen middle. "If you're very quiet, you may even feel him kick."

Henry's countenance brightened. "Him?"

"I have a hunch."

He smoothed her belly with one hand and leaned down and rested his forehead on hers. "I have missed you."

"I'm surprised you can stand to look at me. I must be a sight—"

"Don't do that." He tipped her chin so she met his gaze. "True and spotless, remember? Are you forgetting who you are with?"

Her mouth went dry. "Henry, where were you all this time?"

His hand wrapped around to cup her jaw. "I came after you and I injured my leg. It became infected and I stopped by the next house to ask for help. As it turned out, it was a mad house. The woman who ran it was about as insane as the ex-convicts who stopped there. They used Brumby for meat and used kindness like a weapon to have me indebted to them."

Shock stole every word from her lips till her mouth gaped wide filled only with silence.

"Eventually I ran away and fortunately Toby came to find me, or I'd hate to think where I'd be."

Without a second thought, Agnes wrapped her arms around Henry's neck. "We have to get out of this place. Tonight. We must run."

"No, Agnes," he whispered against her hair, "we tried that, and it didn't work."

She pulled back, her gaze pleading. "What are you saying?"

"You have to go back to Cascades. Trust me."

Her head shook. "No, no, I can't go back there. They'll take our baby, Henry! I've heard all the stories. I know what they do to unwed mothers."

"We are wed in the eyes of God."

"Well, that doesn't seem to matter to them."

He released a weighted breath. "Which is why I want to do this the right way. I have a plan Agnes, but you have to trust me. Can you do that? Can you trust me?"

～⑤～

Henry watched the moonlight dance over Agnes' features and shimmer in her tear-filled eyes. He knew what he was asking of her. To risk her freedom and the life of their child on a chance that he could make a life for them.

"Please Lord," he whispered in his heart, "please make a way for us to be together and to raise our child."

After a long moment, Agnes nodded once and tears tumbled down her cheeks, lining her face. He hadn't noticed the dirt smears until now, or the way her wedding ring was barely visible on her weathered, mud-stained hands.

"Is there something I can do?" he asked quietly. "Would you like something to eat or drink?"

She peered up at him. "Just hold me."

He braced himself as she melted into him. His arms enfolded her barely-there frame, his own abdomen felt the swelling of hers pressed against it. How could they have come so far only to part now? What if his plan didn't come to fruition?

"God Almighty." He turned his gaze to the skies as he held this fragile woman in his arms. "Help us, Lord. Please, help us... Protect our child, we pray."

Agnes' body shuddered against him, and he felt her tears seep through the sleeve of his shirt. "Amen and amen."

His embrace strengthened around her. "He has hold of our child, Agnes. He has hold of all of us. He has not brought us this far to abandon us now."

She nodded against him, and he prayed she believed him.

"He is your God too, you know..."

"I feel like I never have the right words to say to him. All I do is complain." She stepped away to smooth her hands over her face. "Have you ever read Psalm 88?"

The question took him aback and he couldn't suppress the smile that made its way across his lips. "I am not sure, but I am guessing you have?"

She nodded shyly. *"O Lord God of my salvation, I have cried day and night before Thee. let my prayer come before Thee. Incline Thine ear unto my cry. For my soul is full of troubles and my life draweth nigh unto the grave..."* She stifled a sob. "I have memorized it. Every word."

He felt the wet on his face before he knew he was crying. He sucked in a breath. "Agnes, that's—"

"Rather depressing?"

"I was going to say, beautiful. That is beautiful."

His mouth found hers with a renewed eagerness and he smoothed her tears away with open hands. Henry had seen another glimpse into her soul and his attraction to it was undeniable. She met his zeal, standing on tiptoe to reach up and around his neck. But he swiftly tore himself away and pressed his forehead to hers.

"What's wrong?" Agnes whispered.

Henry knew he had promised himself to this woman before God, but according to the law of this new land they were not husband and wife, and he needed to rectify that before he allowed himself to be carried away.

"I want you to be mine in the eyes of the whole world, Agnes Watson. I do not want us raising our family in a state of fear but freedom. I believe God wants that for us." He stroked her wet cheeks then reached into his waistcoat. He pulled out her tin ticket and reached up to tie the red ribbon around her neck. "So, my lovely one, I need you to trust me now. Trust that the Lord will provide."

Agnes touched the numbered ticket then placed her hands on her middle, fresh tears flowing anew. "I trust you. And I trust Him."

Chapter 28

In the early hours, Henry washed and dressed and made his way from the townhouse down to the lieutenant governor's quarters. He waited by the front door, hat in hand, and watched the sky come to life beyond the Southern Ocean. As first light touched the steeple of St David's cathedral, he rapt on the door. A commotion unfolded beyond the door, stumbling, cursing, and heavy footfalls drawing closer. When the door swung open, a half-dressed man with a dark moustache met him, seemingly unimpressed.

"Good morning, Lieutenant Governor. I have come to apply for a marriage to a convict woman," Henry began brightly.

"Make an appointment."

Henry placed a hand on the door before the man could close it. "You see, I would. Only, until you make time to hear my request, I will come here every morning at dawn."

"I could have you arrested."

"Pray tell, what would be the charge?"

He fumbled over his words then finally muttered, "Disturber of the peace."

"Sir, all I ask is for a moment of your time and consideration of my request."

The lieutenant governor's frown deepened. "There's a fee. It will cost you."

"Of course, how much is the fee?"

He gave him a sideways look. "How much do you have?"

"Enough to make it worth your while, Lieutenant Governor."

Stepping back from the doorway, he grunted. "Come on then. You have ten minutes."

"I am most grateful." Henry sidestepped inside and was led into a modest drawing room with little décor. "Is there a Mrs. Lieutenant Governor?"

"No. Now, tell me what this is all about, Mr..."

"Watson. Henry Watson."

"Very well, Mr. Watson." He sunk into one of the settees and gestured to the one opposite. "I assume you want there to be a Mrs. Watson."

"Yes, her number is 227, an Agnes Archibald. We are wed in the eyes of God, but it seems we were unacquainted with the laws here and would like to legitimize the marriage with the government."

"Are there any children?"

"She is with child."

"I see."

Henry leaned forward in the settee. "Sir, please allow me to be frank with you. Miss Archibald was transported here at Christmastime over a minor crime, and I followed her via a free settler ship. We have fought against all odds to be together, and we very well could have run away together but I would so rather live here in town and raise our child here. Raise a whole family here. Is that not what the government ultimately wants? Women who are reformed of their ways, becoming homemakers and mothers, establishing a new colony—which may I remind you can only happen successfully through procreation—before the French get their hands on it."

A smile twisted the lieutenant governor's lips. "Mr. Watson, what you are asking me to allow usually only occurs after four years of good behavior and in that case a Ticket of Leave may be granted. Why should I make an exception for you?"

Henry searched his own heart for the answer and came up with only one. He silently prayed that it would be enough. "Sir, have you ever loved someone so much you would be willing to do whatever it took to protect them?"

He adjusted himself in the settee and secured the final buttons around his neck. "Mr. Watson, you asked earlier if I have a wife. I do not. Or at least, I do not anymore." He cleared his throat and his tone returned to its natural professionalism. "I will grant the Ticket of Leave for #227, and will approve the marriage you request, under one condition. And if you mention this condition to anyone beyond this room, I will deny it completely."

"Very well. Yes, of course, anything, sir."

His dark gaze fixed on Henry with a mix of admiration and warning. "Never take her for granted."

❧

Agnes staggered through the cold overcast yard, hauling piles of convict clothes that wreaked of bodily fluids. Her throat threatened to lurch any contents her stomach still held. A familiar tightness in her belly returned, and she toppled over just short of the wash basin. Scrounging for the clothes, she winced through the ache in her back, the pull across her middle. Her strength was failing, and she wasn't sure if she could even stand. Around her, other convict women went about their duties, ignoring her struggle, set on their own tasks.

She thought back to the evening that was, and remembered Henry's arms around her, his hands on her face, unafraid to touch her though she was so soiled. She remembered the way he had looked at her and the way he laid his hands on her swollen belly. She remembered how he had prayed over them, over their unborn child.

"Lord, give me strength," she whispered, and staggered to her feet. She shifted the load from the ground to the wash basin. She was reaching for the first item for washing when a pain shot through her. Agnes cried out and doubled over.

Bridget marched across the yard, tutting beneath her breath. "Is it to the hospital with ye again?"

Agnes shook her head, feigning strength, till another pain shot through her body. She faltered, curling up on her side. She felt the blood leave her before she saw it. Her heart thudded in her ears, her chest. "No," she cried. "No, God, please. No..."

"Someone help me!" Bridget shouted across the yard.

Another woman bearing the yellow Cs strode over and together they lifted Agnes and hustled her to the Female Factory hospital.

Agnes sobbed as the sharp pain turned to constant aches and cramps. "No, please, God, no. Please, I beg you, please."

"What happened?" Nurse Tedder met them at the door, leading them to a stark white bed.

"She's bleedin'," Bridget said, ladling a trembling Agnes onto the bed.

Agnes shook her head violently, unbelieving what was happening. Nurse Tedder and Bridget had said it from the beginning, spoken death over her and her baby like a curse. But Agnes remembered Henry's prayers from the night before and rested in the promise that the God who held the universe was holding their sweet boy.

"It's too early," Agnes cried, writhing in the bed. "It's far too early."

"Look at me," Nurse Tedder said, grasping Agnes' hand in her own. "227, look at me."

But her eyes were screwed shut against it all.

"Agnes!"

She fixed her attention on the nurse and bit back the sobs. "I cannot... lose... my child..."

Nurse Tedder nodded in understanding. "I will give you something to calm you down and then I will inspect you, if you give me permission?"

She nodded wearily.

Nurse Tedder squeezed her hand before preparing a tonic. "Agnes, I will do all I can for you and your baby."

"Thank you," Agnes breathed and allowed her body to settle into the bed.

Chapter 29

Henry marched into Cascades Female Factory armed with the letter he needed to free Agnes from her sentence. With Toby waiting by the carriage, he prayed it would only be a matter of moments until they were on their way to their new life.

An ever-present eeriness settled over the yard as he strode past the countless women at work, and he almost barreled straight into the weaselly superintendent. The matron, his wife, was nowhere to be seen.

"Good morning, sir. I have a letter from the lieutenant governor with the intent for a Ticket of Leave for #227."

"Take her," the man muttered and continued on his way, "she's a nuisance in this place. Forever in and out of hospital."

"What?" Dread filled Henry and he spun to take hold of the man's arm. "I beg your pardon, sir, but can you please explain yourself?"

He cringed. "227. She's in the hospital again. All this pregnancy business is such an inconvenience. I suppose it's your doing."

Fury burned beneath Henry's skin as he forced himself to release the man and not take the matter further. "Where is she?"

He pointed weakly in a general direction then continued toward the chapel.

Henry marched through the heart of Cascades Female Factory and found the sign for the infirmary. A willowy nurse met him at the door and angled herself to obstruct his access.

"Excuse me, sir. I cannot let you in here without permission."

"I have a letter from the lieutenant governor," he stated plainly. "Is that permission enough?"

Confusion swept over her face. "May I ask which convict woman you are here to—"

"Agnes Archibald."

"This way, sir."

Screams echoed down the halls, taking him back to his time at the Farraway House. From the corner of his eye, he saw a woman tied to a bed, a bandage across her mouth for her to bite upon.

"We only have one hospital here," the nurse went on, "so we tend to everyone. The ill, the insane, those with child."

He nodded in understanding as he was led to a small dim room with four beds but only one patient.

"This is usually the nurse's quarters, but I wanted her to rest away from the noise."

Henry rushed to Agnes' side. She slept soundly, her hands gently resting on her belly.

"How is she?"

"Stable, sir."

"And the baby?"

"By some miracle, still alive." The nurse sighed. "227—Agnes—was in a great deal of pain and she was bleeding, but it seems she just exerted her body. I examined her internally and as far as I can see everything looks fine."

"Thank you," he breathed. "Can she be moved?"

"So long as she is kept on bed rest, yes, but I don't recommend she be put to any sort of work."

"Nurse, if I have it my way, she will never experience another day's work again."

A smile twitched upon her mouth, and she sighed. "Sir, you must be Henry Watson."

"Yes, how did you—"

"She speaks of little else. I am Nurse Tedder, and may I just say, I am for once happy to be proven wrong."

"Whatever do you mean?"

"Never mind, it's not important." She brushed stray curls from Agnes' forehead. "Look after her, won't you?"

"Of course." Henry reached for the tin ticket that hung around Agnes' neck and carefully untied its ribbon. Placing it in Nurse Tedder's waiting palm, he braced himself and threaded his arms beneath Agnes' body. There was nothing to her. Her frail body curled up against his chest and he carried her past the stares of Cascades' women to the tall gates that held them captive.

The guards nodded and unbolted the weighted locks, and Henry carried Agnes out of Cascades Female Factory and into the bright winter day.

❧

A cool washcloth roused Agnes from the depths of sleep. With bleary eyes she searched the light-filled room. Henry slept in the armchair in the corner and Cherry perched on the bed beside her, wringing the cloth into the bowl of water.

"Ye gave us quite the scare, Archie."

"What happened? Where am I?"

"Yer home, love."

"Home?"

Cherry cast her gaze around the room. "It's a fine place, alright. Yer Mr. Watson did well."

She tensed. "And the baby?"

"Is safe, but ye must rest."

Relaxing into the bed, Agnes sighed.

"Our Toby's just fixing some tea. Would ye care for a cup?"

"Please."

Cherry patted her hand affectionately. "Mr. Watson has been out of his mind worried about ye. He's barely left the room. Ye are a very lucky woman, Archie."

"Blessed," she said softly, catching Cherry's attention as she went to rise. "I am a blessed woman."

"Indeed, ye are."

Agnes curled up on her side and watched Henry softly snoring in the corner. He was disheveled, his hair and attire a mess, but she had never loved him more. She laid a hand on her belly and silently thanked the good Lord for keeping their sweet little one safe.

The following Saturday morning Cherry helped Agnes dress into a new muslin gown in sky blue before the priest from St David's visited the Watson home for an intimate ceremony.

Henry sat in a chair by the bed, dressed in his finest suit, and held Agnes' frail hand. Cherry and Toby acted as the witnesses they ought to have had the first time they wed. And there in the quiet master bedroom, Agnes vowed before God and country to love Henry for the rest of her days, till death did them part.

Chapter 30

SEPTEMBER 1837, VAN DIEMEN'S LAND

Henry paced the length of the hallway while beyond the closed doors of the master bedroom Agnes screamed in pain.

Cherry thundered from the room to fetch fresh water from the kitchen, her apron covered in blood.

Henry eagerly followed. "What is happening? What can I do?"

"Stay out of me way." And within an instant, she had vanished behind those doors once again.

Henry perched on the edge of a chair for a moment until another loud cry from Agnes had him on his feet again, anxiously pacing.

"Lord, protect her," he muttered. "Please Lord, protect her... protect our child..."

"Sir, can I get you some tea?" Toby offered, lingering by the kitchen doorway.

"How can I drink tea at a time like this? I should be in there with her."

"It's just not done, sir."

Henry shook his head. "Blast this ridiculous etiquette. She would want me in there."

"Maybe she'd rather you not," Toby said. "I saw my adopted mother give birth once, and I've never forgotten it."

Henry shot him a glare. "This is different. This is my child. She's my—"

"Hen-ry!" Agnes shrieked.

It was all the permission he needed to burst into the room. He rushed to her side, clasped her white clammy hand with both his own, and stared into her face. He tried not to look at the blood smothering the sheets. "What can I do?"

"Just—" She squeezed his hand until he thought it might break. "Argh!"

"Ye shouldn't be in here, sir," Cherry said. "It's not done."

"To hell with that." He pressed a kiss to Agnes' forehead.

"Push, Archie! You're almost there."

In one final convulsion, Agnes' scream was followed by a baby's cry. Henry caught her as she fell into him, all her strength sapped. Sweat drenched her body and she shivered. He pulled a clean blanket over her.

Meanwhile, the child screamed, showing the strength of its lungs.

"Congratulations, sir," Cherry said, smoothing wet cloths over the child before wrapping it in a snug blanket. "Ye have a daughter."

"A girl?"

"So she is, and a fine one at that."

"Did you hear that?" he whispered to Agnes, tears pricking his eyes. "We have a daughter."

Henry lowered Agnes onto the pillow and kissed her forehead before easing out of the chair. He slowly stepped toward Cherry and the bundle she held, overwhelmed by what he was about to see. A girl, he had never imagined himself with a daughter, and yet here she was. Tiny chestnut ringlets hung damp around her cherub face and a rosebud mouth opened, her small fist rubbing against it.

"She's hungry," Cherry said softly.

"Did you hear that, darling, she's hungry." Henry turned to Agnes who was becoming paler by the moment. "Agnes... Darling..." He rushed to her side, touching her cheek. It was cold. He shook her gently. "Agnes?"

A small moan escaped her bluing lips.

"What's going on?"

"Toby," Cherry called, firm and somber. "Call for the physician. Now."

"Right you are."

Henry took Agnes' hand, rubbing in within his own. "Darling, wake up, sweetheart. Our daughter is hungry."

"Here, let's get her on the breast then I'll fetch some sweet tea for Archie."

Henry stepped back while Cherry unbuttoned Agnes' nightdress and angled the pair so the child could suckle. She placed pillows around them before bunching up the bloodied sheets.

"Just make sure she stays latched, I'll get cleaned up and make the tea."

"I thought this wasn't done. Me being here, I mean."

"Well, ye here now, aren't ye. Might as well put yerself to good use."

By the time the doctor arrived to assess Agnes' condition, the baby had nursed and was sound asleep in Henry's arms. With a silver bowl beneath her arm, the doctor bled Agnes. Henry averted his attention and focused on their daughter's deep blue eyes. He had seen enough blood for one day.

"I fear Mrs. Watson's body has been under far too much exertion to recover," the doctor said solemnly. "If the fever breaks through the night, I believe the worst will be over. In the meantime, it must be kept under control."

Henry ladled his daughter into one arm and rose to his feet. "Thank you, doctor."

The doctor paused before he withdrew. "Please do not be under any false assumptions, Mr. Watson. In these situations, it is best to be prepared for the worst."

"Doctor?"

"If the fever does not break and Mrs. Watson worsens, I fear it will be a sign that the good Lord may take her from this world."

"Agnes is a fighter, Doctor. She will not give up."

He sighed. "That may be true, but one can only fight for so long, Mr. Watson. Good day."

❧

Somewhere between dreams and wakefulness, Agnes heard her baby's cry. Delirium claimed her mind and her eyes rolled back. She was faintly aware of Henry's presence, but the overwhelming exhaustion was too much. She was too weak. Her stubborn determination to survive had followed her since birth, becoming the primary motivation behind every decision, her every step. She had to survive the streets, the prison, the voyage, and then Cascades. She had to survive for Henry. Then, for their baby. Now both were safe, and they had each other. She couldn't fight anymore. Her determination dissipated the moment she knew her baby was safe and well beyond her failing body. She had nothing left to give. Her strength was gone and all that was left was the ghost of Agnes Archibald haunting the body of a frail Mrs. Watson.

"Jesus," her heart whispered, "I'm ready."

She didn't even wince when the doctor cut her for bloodletting, she didn't have the strength. A cool washcloth on her forehead felt soothing and freezing at once. Her skin was on fire, so why was she shivering?

Henry's melodic voice pierced through the void of her mind and spoke directly to her heart. "Agnes, I hope you can hear me. We have a daughter, and she's perfect. Now, I need you to be strong and come back to me. To both of us. Please, darling, please... Please fight for us. I beg of you... Don't let go."

Chapter 31

"Does the wee girl have a name yet?" Cherry asked as she opened the curtains the following morning.

Henry glanced at his grey complexion in the looking glass before peering in on his sleeping daughter. "Not yet."

"Best get onto it."

"I am going to let Agnes choose."

Cherry shuffled over to the bed to feel Agnes' forehead and he knew what she was thinking. At least she had the grace not to speak it aloud. "Very good, sir. I'll make some more broth and try to feed her then. We may need to look into a wet nurse, if—"

"Nothing is going to happen to Agnes," Henry said sternly.

Cherry paused by the door, bit her lip then uttered, "I only meant, if Mrs. Watson's milk isn't enough. She's weak, as ye know. I didn't mean..." She shook her head. "I'll get onto that broth."

He sighed. "Cherry, I'm sorry."

With a reassuring smile, Cherry withdrew and left Henry alone with his wife and child. So far, Cherry had managed to get the child to latch and suckle, but she had a point. Perhaps it was draining Agnes? But surely, a mother would want to feed her own child? He didn't want to think of someone else feeding their daughter and Agnes being well again and resenting him for taking away her ability to nurse. It was all too much. What could he do?

He looked to the bright skies beyond the window. Spring was here and the native blossoms covered the evergreen Van Diemen's Land. How he wished Agnes could see it. How he wished he could feel comfortable to venture outside and show his daughter this new world without risking their last moments with her mother.

"Lord, what do I do? You can't have brought her so far to abandon her now. Please do not abandon her, please help my wife... Please, Lord," he whispered again and again until he barely had the words to utter. And when his own words fell short, he found himself in the pages of God's Word. He remembered Psalm 88, the one Agnes had memorized. He opened the book beside her on the bed and tears trickled from his eyes. He took in the final words of the chapter like they were his own, *"Lover and friend hast Thou put far from me, and mine acquaintance into darkness..."*

When Cherry returned with the broth, she attempted to spoon a little into Agnes' mouth, only to have it seep back out and roll down her jaw. Cherry's countenance shifted from hope to horror. "Archie," she whispered, "ye must eat something, or ye'll have no milk for the baby."

Henry shared a concerned look, then leaned deeper into God's Word, his line of sight trailing across to Psalm 89.

"I will sing of the mercies of the LORD for ever. With my mouth will I make known Thy faithfulness to all generations. For I have said, Mercy shall be built up for ever. Thy faithfulness shalt Thou establish in the very heavens..." He released a shuddered breath, travelling over the words in his mind, before whispering aloud, *"And the heavens shall praise Thy wonders, O LORD..."* He turned his attention to his wife barely breathing beside him. *"Thy wonders..."*

It was nothing short of miraculous that he and Agnes were here at all. Two people from different lives, journeying across the world and finding one another once more, and somehow creating new life together. Their daughter was the most wonderful part of it all. Part Agnes, part Henry, she represented all that had been and all that would be for the future. Who would have thought, such tangible hope, such divine grace, could be wrapped up in one so small.

Henry reached for Agnes' pale cold hand and kissed it then pressed it against his stubble lined jaw. "I lost hope once before, Agnes Watson. Never again." Determination set in his eyes, and he watched her intently. "Come back to me. Jesus raised Lazarus from the tomb, and He can save you too. Let Him take over. Let Him be your strength, my dearest Agnes... please."

That afternoon, the doctor visited only to confirm there was nothing to be done but wait. "She's in God's hands now, Mr. Watson."

Henry finally conceded for Cherry to seek out a wet nurse for his unnamed daughter, while Agnes fluttered between night terrors and peaceful sleep. His Bible lay open on the bed beside her, open to the Psalms which

Henry had taken to reading over her daily. He refused to leave her side, except to hold the baby. So often their sweet girl slept in his arms, but he could not bring himself to mind. She was a living breathing thriving miniature of her mother, and he would treasure her every moment he was able. When his exhaustion grew too much to bear however, he placed the sweet one in her cot and lay down beside Agnes, his warm hand over her cold one and prayed. Days upon days of fever and loss of blood, she was now more grey than white, and he wondered if they still even had days left together, or whether it was merely hours.

Somewhere in his exhaustion, he fell into a deep sleep, only to wake again in sheer panic. He lurched upright in the bed and stared at Agnes, watching for the slight rise and fall of breaths. Upon seeing a faint breath, he sighed and relaxed back into the mattress.

"You won't be any good to your daughter if you die too," Toby said from the armchair in the corner, holding the baby in his arms.

Henry shot him a glare. "You're speaking out of place."

But Toby proved unaffected by the statement. "There's tea on the table there. Have some, sir, for all our sakes."

"Thank you," he muttered, rolling out of the bed and taking a cup. "How is she? The baby, I mean?"

"Oh, she's just grand, sir. She was stirring a little so Cherry sent me in while she prepared the feeding bottle."

"Feeding bottle?"

"Yes, sir. She purchased a goat in town and has been milking it for the little one."

"What happened to the wet nurse we hired?"

"Well, sir, we could fetch her if you want but Cherry found this glass bottle at the store especially for infants. In the shape of a submarine no less, and the little one has taken to it quite well."

"Why—" He swung his legs to the side of the bed. "Why would she do that?"

"Well, if Miss Agnes were to get better, of course. Then at least she could feed the baby. Cherry thought it was better than—"

Henry's face twisted and he hung his head, attempting to battle the emotions threatening to consume him.

"I'll leave you alone, sir." Toby stood quietly and carried the baby toward the door. "Cherry can feed her in the drawing room."

Henry stifled a sob. "Very good."

And as the door softly closed, Henry's aching cry burst from his chest. His head fell into his hands. Convulsing in sobs, he strained for breath. What more could he do? He read God's Word over Agnes. He prayed over her. He hoped against hope when the doctor said there was nothing to be done, and he was exhausted. What more could he do? He was trying—

Stop trying.

The voice in his spirit forced him into stillness.

Rest now.

Releasing a final shuddering breath, Henry drank the cold tea then curled up once more against Agnes. He watched the faint breaths leave her lips and he realized how much she would hate this—being vulnerable to the world. She had never wanted to be vulnerable, to be used. She was so accustomed to being strong, to protecting herself and surviving. This must be killing her inside.

All this time his greatest fear had been losing her all over again, but only now did he realize how selfish he was being. Gazing at his beloved wife through bloodshot eyes, he prayed the words he never dared pray before, "Lord, Your will be done. If this is her time, then please let her rest in peace... I am not afraid anymore..."

Chapter 32

Agnes stirred from a nightmare, weak and trembling. Her eyes rolled to see Henry asleep soundly in the bed beside her, his hand upon hers, his Bible open between them. She didn't even have the strength to squeeze his hand, to tell him she was there. She licked her dry lips, praying for relief, and Cherry was at her side within moments.

"Archie," she whispered, and Agnes found comfort in the hope in her tone. "Yer awake."

Her throat felt so coarse. She couldn't speak.

"Oh here, love, here have some of this." Cherry took a spoonful of broth and gently ladled it into Agnes' parched mouth. It trickled through her body like honey, its herbs and spices bringing her awake. Again, Cherry helped Agnes drink the broth from the spoon, until Agnes could finally part her lips and find her words.

"How is the baby?"

"Oh, she's just fine, Archie."

"She?"

"Yes, ye have a fine girl on yer hands, Archie. And Mr. Watson is most besotted with her. Ye just wait until ye see them together."

"May I see her now?"

"Of course. Let me fetch Toby, he is just giving her the feeding bottle."

It didn't make much sense but if the baby was well and fed that was all that mattered. Within moments, Cherry returned with the tiny infant in her arms.

"Now, let's just undo yer nightdress a bit so she can feel you. It'll help both of ye." Cherry smiled and discreetly undid the top buttons with one hand and then eased the baby onto Agnes' chest, careful to still steady her.

Agnes gazed down into the sweet face of their daughter. Part Henry, part Agnes, this child had wild curls and her father's eyes. Tiny fingers scratched at Agnes' chest as the baby nuzzled her.

Cherry looked apologetic. "Oh, she must still be hungry."

"May I try?" Agnes asked softly.

"Of course, but please don't be disheartened if—"

"I won't," Agnes promised. "I'd just like to try."

Cherry nodded and helped Agnes with her nightdress and then to latch the baby onto Agnes' breast.

"Oh." Agnes flinched at the baby's eagerness and was surprised when she didn't let go and wail.

"Well, she must be getting something," Cherry laughed. "Which is nothing short of a miracle, Archie."

Still weary, Agnes' eyes fluttered closed as she relished in the warmth of her little one upon her chest. She wasn't sure what had transpired but somehow the terrors of the night had broken, and, in that moment, she remembered the prayer of Elizabeth Fry upon her departure.

...May she discover the light of our Lord and Savior Jesus Christ in dark places, and may she experience the wonder of Your grace...

Henry roused beside her, drowsy and grey. He rolled toward her only for his eyes to fly open at the sight of her nursing their daughter. "Agnes," he breathed, "how—"

He cupped her face, kissing her cheek, her lips, her forehead then rested his head against hers. "I thought I'd lost you."

"I thought so too," Agnes said softly. "But look, she's feeding."

He beamed and smoothed the baby's soft chestnut curls.

"What's her name?" Agnes asked.

"She doesn't have one yet. I wanted you to choose."

"You knew I would be all right?"

"I hoped, and by God's grace you are."

Tears stung Agnes' eyes and spilled over her cheeks. "Her name is Beth, after Mrs. Fry."

Henry's face twisted as he seemed to fight his own rising tears. "It's perfect."

❧

The day Beth Watson was christened in St David's church, Henry held her with one arm, and steadied Agnes with the other. His wife became stronger by the day and Beth grew brighter and chubbier. He could not remember a time he was more at peace than in Hobart Town and he finally understood what it meant to be free in Christ. It was not because they had been free to marry or that Agnes' Ticket of Leave meant she could live out her sentence beneath his roof and as his wife. Rather, the bondage that had claimed him since childhood, the terrors that had haunted that young Master Watson trailing the streets of London, first, searching for his mother who had run away from his father when Henry was only five, and then finding Josephine the way he had at age twelve, it had all come to an overwhelming halt the moment he had to choose to let Agnes go. The Lord gave and the Lord took away, but thankfully, he did not take her away that day. And Henry would forever remember the stern warning the lieutenant governor had given him all those months ago—never to take his wife for granted. Lord help him, he prayed he never would.

Beth's first Christmas proved bright and sunny. Cherry decorated the townhouse with eucalyptus branches and red bottlebrush flowers, and Toby cut a fresh South Esk pine tree for the drawing room which Agnes thrived in decorating.

It was Agnes' first real Christmas in a long time, so Henry wanted to make it special. He replaced her old wedding band with a solid gold one. Beth received knitted booties and blankets for when the cooler weather struck, and Cherry and Toby were both gifted a handsome sum to spend however they chose.

When the grandfather clock chimed midnight, and Beth had long been asleep, Agnes and Henry escaped the festivities for their own intimate celebration. Their time together before had been brief, they barely had gotten acquainted with one another before they were separated again. Then, it took time for Agnes to heal. Tonight, however, Henry's Christmas present lay waiting in their marital bed, where they could finally be one without fear. Lost in wonder.

Acknowledgements

This book wouldn't exist without my dear friend Jennifer Q. Hunt, to whom it is dedicated. When I reached out to her raving about my latest historical find, she told me I *had* to write this story. She never questioned my ability to write historical fiction—something I do constantly—she just believed I could. And so I did. Jennifer, thank you for being the initial sounding board of this idea and for your gentle guidance in so many ways.

Thank you to my fellow Christian Mommy Writers for your endless support and especially to Dani Renee for your feedback in those early stages.

Thank you to Jenny Glazebrook for your encouraging words and to Wendy Parker for your constant prayers over my journey as a writer. You are both invaluable to me.

To my husband, thank you for insisting I purchase the research book rather than borrow it from the library—that book was not fit to be seen let alone read by another person by the time I was finished with it. And thank you for believing in my writing. It's your support that makes this possible.

Lastly, but most importantly, thank you to my Lord and Savior Jesus Christ, who not only gives me the freedom to live as a child of God but calls me on this great adventure with Him, to partner with Him in creativity. You have my heart forever.

About the Author

Liz Chapman is a Jesus-loving mama who loves to write. Theology, history, and tea are a few of her passions, but her favorite time is spent with her toddler sidekick, sweet baby, and spunky coffee-connoisseur of a husband.

Liz has a Graduate Diploma in Creative Writing and is currently studying for a Master of Divinity. She is also the founder of DOLL Ministries.

Her other works include *Azure Blaze*, the first book of the Spirit Flame series, published under her pseudonym Elizabeth C. Natalia.

For more information or to contact the author visit
www.theworshipdesk.com

YELLOW HEART

love stories to strengthen and inspire

DOLL Ministries' mission with Yellow Heart Book Series is to publish love stories with characters who experience the battle to follow Christ in hopes that it might strengthen and inspire others in their faith.

For more information visit
www.dollministries.com